OUT OF UKRAINE

Emily Gallo

Cover design by Alice Graham
Instagram@alicegonedigital

The author may be reached at
ecegallo@gmail.com

www.emilygallo.com
http://emilygallo.blogspot.com/

Other novels by Emily Gallo:

Venice Beach
The Columbarium
Kate & Ruby
Roads not Taken
Murder at the Columbarium
The Last Resort
DREAMer
Bardo

Thank you to my incredible editors, Daniel Nauman and Chris Saur and my husband David Gallo for their continued support and help in creating all my books.

And thanks to the Tin Roof Café where I have written all my books over cups of Earl Grey Tea.

"Ms. Gallo has expertly intertwined social issues and current topics of the day through the story like a skilled weaver, creating a masterpiece that is filled with emotion, suspense, empathy, and love for others."
InD'tale Magazine

"The contrast between tone and content is a characteristic talent of only a few authors. Gallo pays as much attention to her sentences as she does her plots, shifting or consolidating meaning with the use of a single word. Her writing is impeccably honed, full of juxtapositions and qualifications that help to create an authentic and emotional atmosphere throughout."
Goodreads Review

"Emily Gallo transports the reader into all her books. Filled with well defined characters and an intriguing storyline, the books are hard to put down."
Amazon Review

For Jojo

1

Winter 2020

HEATHER CAME INTO THE BEDROOM FROM THE ADJOINING BATH WITH TEARS IN HER EYES. Eric bit his lip, slid off the bed and got up to hug her. He sighed and murmured, "Another negative?"

Heather nodded and let the tears flow. "I don't know how much longer I can do this," she sobbed. "It wasn't like this with Chloe."

"That was a long time ago, when you—*we* were a lot younger," he replied softly, kissing the top of her head. Heather exhaled loudly and fell onto the bed. She closed her eyes and pictured their daughter as an infant and a toddler . . . before she developed the cancer that eventually killed her. He lay down next to her. "Maybe you should make an appointment with the Ob-Gyn," he said quietly. "Maybe something's wrong that can be fixed."

"But why would something be wrong now? I didn't have trouble getting pregnant with Chloe."

Eric rolled his head on the comforter. "I don't know, but you did have a lot of issues during the pregnancy."

"Maybe it's you," she retorted.

"I'm willing to explore that." He studied the ceiling and added, "I'm also willing to explore adoption."

"I don't want to talk about adoption yet."

"Heather, be realistic—"

"I said *yet*. I'm not ruling it out. I just think we should see what the doctor says and if there's anything else we can do."

"And I said *explore*." They sighed simultaneously. "Let's not argue," he continued. "We're stressed out. Three years of negative results. Let's give it a rest. Make an appointment with the doctor and ask him if I should get tested." He got up and started to leave the bedroom.

"Maybe we need to try fertility treatments," Heather called after him.

Eric turned around and faced her. "Call the doctor and see what he says."

That evening over dinner, Heather told Eric about her phone call with the doctor. "He said there are different things to try. There's a tubal flush and a drug called Letrozole. I also did some Googling and found people who said acupuncture and Chinese herbs worked for them." Eric looked at her skeptically. "Shouldn't we try everything we can?" she pleaded.

"Did you make an appointment?"

"Yes. Next Tuesday."

Eric nodded. "Let's wait until then." Heather started to reply, but she knew Eric well enough. One step at a time, she thought. But that didn't stop her from spending hours searching the Internet for anything related to infertility.

Heather and Eric sat in front of Doctor Morris at his desk on Tuesday. "There are some abnormalities, but I think it's more about your age and your health, Heather. You've been trying for how long?"

"About three years," Heather replied.

Dr. Morris nodded and frowned. "I think it's time to look into IVF. But really, Heather, I'm not sure you can or should carry a baby yourself."

"What do you mean?" Eric asked.

"Heather, you are over forty. You had problems during the other pregnancy, especially during delivery, and you were in your thirties then. If you can afford it, you might look into surrogacy."

"Whoa," Eric cut in. "You mean have someone else carry the baby?"

"Yes. It will still be your baby. It will be your sperm and her eggs. We combine them in the lab and then implant one or more into the surrogate."

Heather and Eric were silent, both processing the news. "But why can't I get pregnant?" Heather asked. "We didn't have trouble with Chloe."

"There'd have to be much more extensive testing to answer your question. And even then, we can't always find the reason."

"What about that medication? Or fallopian tubal flush?"

Dr. Morris shook his head. "As I said, it's risky and not foolproof. IVF is the best alternative."

Heather started to cry and Eric put his arm around her. "Um," Eric said, looking over at the doctor, "we'll have to talk about it."

"Let me give you some information about the whole IVF process which is what my office can help you with." Dr. Morris left the room and returned with some pamphlets. "You can look into surrogacy online and then call me when you've had a chance to familiarize yourself with the process."

They stood on the sidewalk outside the Doctor's office as Heather tried to control her crying. Eric finally kissed her on the cheek. "I'm sorry, but I have to get to work. We'll talk about it tonight." He squeezed her shoulders and turned toward the Embarcadero to catch the Muni.

Heather went into a coffee shop to gather her thoughts. She took out her phone and spent the next hour or so Googling IVF and surrogacy after glancing through the pamphlets.

It was all so overwhelming . . . and would take much more time than she wished. And, of course, even this process wasn't a sure thing.

She would have to take some medication before starting the actual process to help her ovaries produce viable eggs. But Dr. Morris had said that her ultrasound and blood test showed that her ovaries were healthy, so maybe she wouldn't have to do it for long. She took out a post-it note pad and started writing questions to ask the doctor and to discuss with Eric.

There were several fertility centers in the San Francisco area with varying success rates and varying costs. Most of them hovered in the twenty to thirty-five percent rate of success for a woman just over 40 using non-donor eggs and that was about the national average. That was a bit of a letdown. Heather wrote down the name of two that had rates over thirty-five percent.

The costs also differed widely, ranging from $8,000 to $35,000, although there were ways to cut costs. Some of them required taking more medication than others and the medication was a few thousand on top of the cost of the procedure itself. And all of that is before the cost of surrogacy, which is the most expensive part of the process."

She even looked at a few clinics in southern California near where her parents lived. She could conceivably go to one there and stay at her parents' house during the two to three weeks for the procedure if she found one down there with a high success rate.

That evening they sat over dinner discussing the pros and cons. "I didn't realize the success rates were so low," Eric said.

Heather frowned. "I guess some people have to do it more than once. The one near my parents uses a bit of a different protocol and they use less meds. Also, some of them are geared toward older patients."

"But two to three weeks with your parents?" Eric sniffed. Heather managed a little grin. "I mean there have to be similar opportunities here in the Bay Area."

Heather sighed. "There are, but some of them with better success rates actually only take patients who have a better chance at success so the rates are kind of skewed."

"So how do we decide?"

"I guess we need to rank them in some way."

"It's going to be so expensive, no matter what," Eric sighed. "It's not like I can squeeze more money out of the nonprofit I work for."

"You do have that job offer with that tech company."

Eric put his fork down. "Even with that I don't think we can afford it."

Heather's lips drew a thin line. "Dr. Morris didn't make it sound like I had a choice."

2

A WEEK OR TWO LATER ERIC AND HEATHER WERE FINISHING DINNER WHEN ERIC'S PHONE RANG. He glanced at it and answered. "Hi Mom. Okay. Saturday?" He looked over at Heather, who shrugged. "Green River Taproom at one. See you then." He hung up. "You know that place in Winters? The one with all the beer taps on the wall? Mom and Brian want to ride their bikes there from Davis if weather permits, and asked if I'd meet them there. Want to come?"

"I can't on Saturday. I have to finish up with that client for the blue jean ad." She paused, thinking about her final layout. "But say hi to your Mom and step-dad for me."

"I will."

Heather tapped her fingers on the table.

"Eric, I want to try this."

Eric stopped picking up the dishes off the table. "IVF?"

"I need your support."

"You have my support," he replied with a sigh, resuming clearing the table. "It's just . . ."

"The cost. I know. I can hope for more and better clients along with a baby."

Eric managed to chuckle as he held the pile of dishware to his chest. "Okay, babe. Even if we have to beg, steal—"

Heather lunged toward him. "I love you!"

Eric teetered back and laughed. "Watch out! We gotta make these dishes last now."

Brian and Abby met Eric at the Green River Taproom and they all wandered along the wall, gathering beer tastes. They found a table and started sampling. "I kind of like this pilsner," Abby said. She looked at Eric, who stared at his beers as if he didn't know where to start. "You seem preoccupied," she continued. "Is everything okay?"

"I suppose. Well, you know, we've been trying for another baby for quite awhile . . . and we're at the point of looking into IVF and surrogacy."

"Huh?" Brian asked.

"In vitro fertilization. My sperm and Heather's egg in a petri dish."

"I like the old fashioned way better," Brian smirked.

Abby gave him a dirty look and turned back to Eric. "Why surrogacy?"

Eric shrugged. "The doc thinks it would be difficult for Heather to carry the baby."

Abby turned back to Brian with a calculating gaze. He managed to look abashed as he took another sip of beer. "I've heard it's very expensive," she finally said to no one in particular.

"It sure is. We'll both have to squeeze more out of our careers. It's a lot to take in, I know, but Heather wants to do it. The doctor said because of her age and all her problems during Chloe's pregnancy . . ." Eric's voice trailed off.

"You said Heather wants to do it. How about you?"

Eric shrugged. "I don't know. It just seems a little weird."

Abby touched her son's arm. "It'll still be your baby." Eric nodded and smiled half-heartedly.

"How do you go about finding a surrogate?" Brian asked.

"There are agencies. They take care of almost everything. I don't know much of the details yet. We need to decide what fertility clinic to use. We still have a lot of research to do before we begin."

Abby nodded and looked back at Brian. He blinked and coughed and then pushed back his chair. "Shall we toast?" He lifted his glass and Eric and Abby followed suit. "Here's to our new grandchild." Abby and Eric glanced at each other. She knew her son was still on the fence, but she was grateful to Brian for putting a positive spin on it.

"Thank you, Brian," Abby beamed. "That was lovely." She fumbled in her purse and pulled out her phone. "Now I need to text your sister Paige, and tell her the good news. She'll be thrilled too."

"Aw, Mom," Eric sighed. "Maybe it's a little too early for that."

"I know. I know," she replied, giving him a reassuring pat on the knee. "I'll just say you two are *considering* it."

Heather was nowhere to be found when Eric got home. He glanced at his phone, but there were no notifications from her. He went to his computer and started looking up agencies for surrogacy and found the prices even more than he had expected. California was a state that allowed them, but like everything else in California, they were over-the-top expensive. Oregon was another western state that allowed it, but most of the others were in the Midwest, South or East. And it was still very expensive, even there. He looked at other countries and found that Europe did not allow it and neither did Canada or Australia. He closed his computer and started to text Heather to ask where she was, but then she arrived. "How are your mom and Brian?" she asked as she flopped onto the couch.

"Good."

"Did you tell them about our plans?"

"Yes. Like us, my mom wondered how we would afford it."

Heather closed her eyes. "We'll figure it out."

"Heather, where are we going to get that kind of money?"

"Dip into our retirement? Sell stocks? Refinance the house?" She opened her eyes and almost glared at him. "There are ways, Eric."

He grimaced and changed the subject. "What'll we have for dinner?"

Heather shrugged. "I'm not hungry right now. I had a big lunch with my client."

"I'll just make a sandwich then." Eric escaped to the kitchen. He made his dinner and took it to the living room, finding it empty. He turned on the television to get his mind onto something else.

About an hour later Heather returned from her office. "I did some research. There are other countries where surrogacy is legal and much cheaper. I'm going to call some places on Monday and see what I can find out."

"Um hmm," Eric replied. He then raised his eyebrows. "Have you told your parents yet?"

"Not yet."

"What do you think they'll say?"

"Probably same as yours . . . that it's so expensive. I think I'll wait to find out about these other countries before I tell them." She managed a smile. "That way I'll have a comeback."

"Good idea."

On Monday Heather spent the morning researching online and found several agencies and gathered as much information as she could to present to Eric and to her parents. She also called Dr. Morris' office to get more information about the IVF process. It was a busy morning, but she felt confident that the information she had received would help ease Eric's concerns. And give her ammunition to tell her parents who she was hoping might offer to help pay for some of it. She knew they wouldn't be on board with this right away. She wanted to give them time to accept it before asking for money. Actually, she hoped they would just offer.

Heather brought all the notes she had taken to the dinner table to share with Eric. "I think our best bet will be Ukraine."

Eric held his forkful of salad midair. "So far away?!"

"But affordable and they are part of the European Union now."

"Wow. Not a country I ever thought I'd be visiting."

"Oh, it'll be fun and interesting."

"I guess," he replied, dropping the salad on his plate.

Eric called his mother after dinner to tell her what they had decided. "Ukraine? My goodness!" Abby responded. "Have you set it up already?"

"Heather's working on all that. She's been emailing one of the coordinators who works with several agencies. Then we'll choose an agency that he recommends, trying to get as much information as possible before starting the IVF cycle. And it's about a third the cost of doing it here."

"Where does she do this?"

"We're not sure yet."

"Well, I guess it's really happening!" Abby exclaimed.

"I guess so." Eric hung up and took a deep breath. His mother was right. It's really happening.

3

JED ARRIVED AT THE COLUMBARIUM EARLIER THAN USUAL TO PREPARE FOR A NINE AM MEMORIAL. He unlocked the gates and set out chairs and an easel in the atrium and cleaned the niche (or apartment, as Jed liked to call them) that would hold the ashes. The family arrived about fifteen minutes before nine and set the photo on the easel. "Do you have any idea how many people will be coming?" Jed asked. "I set up fifty chairs."

"Oh I doubt more than that," the woman's son answered. "Probably not even twenty people will show up. After all, she was ninety-six and all her friends are gone by now. It'll just be the family and there aren't that many of us."

Jed nodded. "Will you want music?"

The son shook his head. "No. It'll be a short and sweet service. She had Alzheimer's and didn't even know any of us for the last few years.

It's kind of like she already died. I know it sounds crass . . ."

"Oh no, I get it," Jed said, patting the man's back. "Did you bring things to put inside the apartment with her ashes?"

"My sister has them."

"Okay. I'll meet you at the apartment when you're done with the service."

As the few family and friends arrived, they all commented with oohs and aahs at the gorgeous domed building with its stained glass windows, marble floor, balconies and pillars. The neoclassical building had alcoves on each floor filled with glass-doored niches. One of the attendees plucked at Jed's sleeve. "How many floors are there?"

"We have three stories with over eight thousand apartments." Jed smiled. "I call the smaller niches, apartments and the larger ones, condos. I'd be happy to give you a tour and tell you the history of the building, as well as a little about some of our residents if you want to come back sometime."

"I'd like that. I can see that some of these, um, apartments, have interesting artifacts. I've never seen anything like this. It's much more special to bury loved ones this way instead of a hole in the ground and a cement block as a marker." Jed nodded and turned to welcome other guests as they arrived.

The service was indeed short and sweet, and Jed and the family met at the apartment on the third floor. They added a few mementos, a couple of photos, and the urn filled with the ashes. "Thanks, Jed," the son called out as the family members descended the stairs. "We'll see you soon when we come for a visit."

Jed was soon back into the rhythm of the day-to-day activities of the columbarium. As he swept one of the alcoves, he saw a familiar couple standing in front of a niche. "Eric! Heather!" Jed called out as he approached them. "Do you have something new to put in Chloe's apartment?"

"Hi Jed," Heather said. "No. We just have some news to tell Chloe . . . and you." Heather and Eric glanced at each other. "We tried to conceive after Chloe died but we couldn't get pregnant. Anyway, the doctor suggested we try IVF."

"What is that?"

"In vitro fertilization," Heather responded. "They combine Eric's sperm and my egg in a lab."

"So you're pregnant? That's wonderful!"

"Well, not exactly." Jed looked perplexed. "We're going to use a surrogate."

"A surrogate?"

"I'm over forty and I have some health issues, and I also had a difficult labor and delivery with Chloe. I guess we didn't know it at the time, but—" Heather swallowed hard. "Chloe was our miracle baby."

"The doctor recommended finding a surrogate rather than risk Heather's or the baby's life," Eric added quickly.

"I see."

"It's expensive to get a surrogate here in the United States—like over a hundred and fifty thousand dollars."

Jed's eyes popped. "Wow!"

"So we're looking into doing it in other countries where it's cheaper, like Georgia, Colombia or Ukraine."

"Georgia? I thought you said it was too expensive in the United States."

"Oh, not the state of Georgia," Heather explained. "Georgia the country, near Russia."

"Well," chuckled Jed. "Learn something new every day. My world's pretty small here," he said, waving his arm around.

"And we're so glad you're here," smiled Heather.

"Columbia and Mexico were cheaper than the US, but about the same as Georgia or Ukraine," Eric continued, very much in calculating mode. "In both Georgia and Ukraine, though, our names would be on the birth certificate; the surrogate's would not. And the process of getting the baby home with an American passport is a fairly easy procedure. Georgia however has a lower quality of medical care than Ukraine."

"So you're doing it in Ukraine?"

"Yeah."

"And that's—"

"Not far from Georgia," explained Heather.

"So far away."

"About six thousand miles and ten hours ahead," Eric went on. "And thirteen hours in an airplane."

"Do you have to stay in Ukraine the whole time?"

"Oh no. We do the IVF here and then a courier service takes it to Ukraine for implanting in the surrogate."

"Sounds like science fiction," Jed murmured. "How long will it take?"

"At least a year after we start the IVF cycle, I think," Heather answered. "It depends on a lot of factors, including whether or not the first implantation takes."

Jed nodded and smiled. "I'll leave you alone now to tell Chloe about her soon-to-be new brother or sister." He hugged them both. "Keep me posted."

Jed went downstairs and found his mind wandering to how Chloe and his own daughter, Genevieve, were both four years old when they died. It had taken him years and years of anger and grief before he could even function. He had promised Eric and Heather when they put Chloe in her apartment that he would watch over her. He sang to her every morning as well as several of the other residents who had been special to him. He had never shared with Eric and Heather how taking care of Chloe's ashes had actually helped him accept Genevieve's death and move past it, but it was true.

Then he thought about the celebration of life he had just witnessed and how that's the way it's supposed to be. Chloe and Genevieve's deaths had disrupted the circle of life . . . four-year olds aren't supposed to die, leaving their parents grieving.

Meanwhile, Heather and Eric stood silently at Chloe's niche or apartment, holding hands and letting their tears come. They opened the apartment and spoke softly to Chloe as they held the teddy bear that had been placed inside. After several minutes they went downstairs and out to their car. Eric turned the radio to NPR and the news. "This virus in Wuhan China has now killed seventeen and sickened five hundred," the news anchor stated. "China has Wuhan under quarantine, as well as placed a restricted access protocol on Huanggang, thirty miles from Wuhan. That's 18 million people on lockdown."

"Jeez! That's crazy!" Eric said.

"But no one has it here in the U.S., right?"

"I think there are a few cases."

"Well, I didn't want to go to Wuhan anyway," Heather teased. They both laughed and squeezed each other's hand, happy to see that they could actually kid around after paying a visit to Chloe. Perhaps the idea of a new baby would help them get past their grief after all.

4

Spring 2020

WHILE HEATHER WAS RESEARCHING FERTILITY CLINICS AND ERIC WAS APPLYING FOR NEW JOBS, THE WORLD HEALTH ORGANIZATION ISSUED A GLOBAL HEALTH EMERGENCY. Global air travel became restricted and most countries, the United States included, declared Covid-19 a public health emergency. A cruise ship had twenty-one positive cases so no country allowed them to dock, and WHO declared Covid a pandemic. San Francisco and all of California had gone into a statewide lockdown soon after that when cases soared.

Heather had narrowed it down to one clinic near her parents' house and one in San Francisco. There were pros and cons for both. Their success rates were similar but the one in San Francisco was more expensive and their protocol included using more meds, so Heather opted to go to the one in southern California. She had finally talked to her parents about having IVF and they had encouraged her to come there to have it done. They offered to help with the cost and that became an important factor in the decision.

Eric would drive her down to her parents' house and deposit his sperm the same day they did the egg retrieval surgery on Heather. The process was supposed to take just a few weeks, if all went well. They would then freeze the embryos in order to send them to Ukraine to be implanted into a surrogate's uterus.

Eric took a new job in the tech industry. It paid a great deal more than his previous job at the nonprofit, but he wasn't happy about the change. Most of the other employees were half his age. They needed to get more money for the IVF and surrogacy, however, as well as to make up for the money they'd lose when Heather took maternity leave. He would need to work remotely when they would be traveling to Ukraine to pick up the baby, and that was more the standard of tech companies. He wasn't a techie, but he was personable, so he took a position in the sales sector of the company.

Meanwhile Heather had been getting ready to start the process soon. But then everything changed when California issued a statewide stay-at-home order. The columbarium closed, but Jed still went in almost every day to check on things and was there to answer the phone several weeks later when Heather called. "Heather! Great to hear from you."

"Oh, hi Jed. I didn't expect you to answer. I was just calling to see if the columbarium was open."

"The columbarium is closed, but I've got plenty to do around here anyway. How's everything going?"

"We found a fertility clinic in southern California near my parents, but we're waiting until things settle down with Covid. I'm kind of worried about going anywhere. I want to make sure I'm healthy before starting the medication I need to take before the egg retrieval."

"I've heard that the whole healthcare system is crushed by Covid patients and they discourage people from going to hospitals for anything else."

"And there are shortages of protective gear," Heather added. "I know we are all supposed to be masked with those N-95s, but there aren't enough even for hospital personnel."

"So how are you and Eric doing during this Covid pandemic?"

"Driving each other crazy, trying to work from home!"

Jed laughed. "Well, that's better than getting Covid."

"True. How about you and your wife—is it Monica?"

"Monica and I are fine as of now. She too is working from home so I come here to get out of her hair."

"I wish I had somewhere to go! I'll let you know when we have news."

"You and Eric take care." They hung up.

Heather was refocusing on a new project when Eric walked in. "Who was that?"

"Jed. I was just updating him."

"Oh, how's he doing?"

"He's at the columbarium even though it's closed down."

"All that maintenance . . ." Eric murmured. And then he smiled. "And he has to sing to Chloe and the others."

Heather managed to smile back. "It is a comfort knowing he's watching over Chloe."

Eric sighed. "This fertility process is so long and maddening. And now this damn Covid makes things even more difficult."

Heather looked out the window. "It's our only chance."

"We could have adopted—"

"Eric! Please don't start." Eric frowned and left the room. Heather went back to her drawing, but her attention kept wandering to all that loomed ahead of them. They had taken quite a while to start thinking about choosing the surrogate. Eric had been very scrupulous and Heather worried that he wasn't a hundred percent on board. She knew he was doing this for her, but she also knew he would be a great father once the baby arrived. He had been that to Chloe.

They didn't talk about it for a while, waiting for things to finally reopen. Things did not get better with Covid, however. Instead they got a lot worse. Masks were required in public everywhere, not that there were many places to go. Almost all indoor venues were closed including restaurants, gyms, and churches . . . only essential businesses like grocery stores were allowed to stay open. Glass partitions were put up at cash registers and no one was allowed in without a mask. All schools were closed so children had to do their work from home via computer as did parents who had the kind of jobs that allowed it. Prisons were releasing prisoners early because of the mounting cases there. They even closed some parks and beaches in California. Covid cases were soaring and hospitals were unable to treat all the patients. The United States surpassed Italy and Spain as the country with the most cases.

Heather found a few places online where people chatted about their experiences and that was extremely helpful in relieving her anxiety about the whole situation. She used their recommendations to narrow down her agency search. She found a coordinator, Luka, who worked with a few different agencies in Ukraine and he was very helpful. They finally settled on an agency and put down their five thousand dollar deposit.

5

Winter 2021

ERIC WAS FOCUSING ON HIS JOB AND HAD PUSHED HIS APPREHENSION ABOUT SURROGACY AND IVF FAR DOWN ON HIS LIST OF CONCERNS. It was bad enough that he didn't really like his new job, but having to work from home because of the lockdown made it even more difficult. He was a salesman and person-to-person contact was key to making sales. Zoom meetings just weren't the same.

The good news was that a couple of pharmaceutical companies had finished enough clinical trials for vaccines against Covid that they had started giving them out free in December. The vaccines, however, were only to be given to healthcare personnel, people over seventy-five, and people in long-term care facilities in the first phase. The bad news was that California postponed reopening because cases had surpassed three million. Not that Heather would have wanted to be vaccinated. She didn't want any possibility of interference with the medication she would be taking. "Could things get any worse?" Heather thought to herself.

Eric and Heather continued to wait to begin the IVF process and had followed the recommendations of the Center for Disease Control, spending Thanksgiving, Christmas and New Years away from family. Covid cases continued to rise worldwide to 100 million with new variants starting to pop up.

"How long are we going to have to wait to do this?" Heather groaned. "This damn Covid!"

Eric wanted to comfort her, but there was nothing he could say. They weren't supposed to travel anywhere and most clinics and hospitals were keeping people away except for emergency procedures. "It can't be too much longer," he finally said.

"Cases and deaths are going up, not down!" Heather snapped back.

"Let's just try to make the best of it," Eric shrugged and sighed.

"We need to get this started," Heather said one morning at breakfast.

"I guess we should," Eric replied. "We're not getting any younger and Covid does not seem to be going away."

"I'm glad you agree because I already called the fertility clinic and made an appointment. I needed to schedule it around my period."

"When's the appointment?"

"Next Monday. I hope you can drive me to my parents' house this weekend. Then we can meet with the doctor and plan the whole thing before you go back. I'll need to stay there for a few weeks . . . at the very least. It depends on how well it goes and when my period starts."

"Why am I the last to know?" Eric asked with a bit of irritation.

"Because I thought you might try to talk me out of it."

"Heather, I'm fine with it now. Really."

She hugged him. "I'm sorry. You're just so preoccupied with work and everything."

Eric kissed her. "It's okay."

The rest of the week was a flurry of activity packing and preparing for Heather to be away for a while. They drove down to southern California on Saturday and spent Sunday enjoying the beach. "I'm pretty nervous," Heather said as they climbed into bed Sunday night.

"Well, tomorrow they'll just be doing tests, right?"

"I know, but what if something's wrong with my uterus?"

"Didn't we already go through the tests with Dr. Morris?"

"We have to do it again because it's been so long."

Eric hugged her. "Just focus on what the outcome will be."

The appointment went well. They both liked the doctor and the clinic and the tests showed them to be healthy and ready. Eric drove back to San Francisco and Heather readied herself for the weeks ahead. She had been meeting with clients over Zoom, so working from her parents' house was not a problem. She started taking the drugs that she had to inject into herself to stimulate the ovaries and prevent premature ovulation. This went on for almost two weeks, and would help her produce as many eggs as possible during this cycle.

The egg retrieval surgery was scheduled for a Friday so that Eric could drive down Thursday after work and be there to produce the sperm in the clinic. The timing had to be very precise for this stage. The surgery was quick and successful and the fertilization process with Eric's sperm had no issues. But they had to wait almost a week to find out how many of the newly created embryos would come to maturity. Heather stayed at her parents' house to be near the clinic, but Eric went back home since his job had started requiring him to come to the office occasionally.

After six stressful days of waiting, Heather and Eric got on a three-way call with the clinic. "You have three mature embryos," the doctor from the clinic said. "Not bad for one round."

"Great news!" Eric said excitedly after the doctor disconnected from the call.

"Sure," Heather replied. "But that means we only have three chances, and we have to send all three to Ukraine and what if something goes wrong?"

"I guess something could," Eric said, his enthusiasm dipping a little bit. "Let's just stay positive."

In March vaccines became available for everyone, regardless of age and some of the masking and social distancing mandates were lifted. Eric got vaccinated, but Heather worried that she might have to go through the process again if something happened in transporting the embryos to Ukraine. She worried about what the vaccine might do to the eggs. She stayed in southern California and got busy making plans to get the embryos shipped. It wasn't easy during the pandemic, but she finally found a company willing to take the frozen embryos in the portable container filled with liquid nitrogen. The courier had a special permit to carry it onto the plane with him rather than leave it in the luggage compartment. It was then handed to the agency in Ukraine.

With Luka's help they had settled on a surrogate and she was vetted both medically and psychologically. After they approved her work-up, they signed the contract and then the agency, the surrogate, and the coordinator all signed it. There were a few more legalities so that process and the transporting of the embryos dragged out a little longer. Then they had to wait for the perfect timing in the surrogate's menstrual cycle to implant the embryo. They had decided to try just one embryo; they didn't want to deal with having twins. They would take their chances and at least there would be two more frozen embryos already there if the first one didn't work.

The day came to implant the embryo, but that was followed by ten excruciating days of waiting before the pregnancy test. Eric went down to pick up Heather so they could be alone together when they heard the news. When the news came, it was not good. The transfer had been unsuccessful. "Oh Eric!" Heather sobbed. "What did I do to deserve this?"

Eric tried to comfort her, but he too felt devastated. "There are two more viable embryos there ready to go as soon as the timing is right."

"I wonder if they can implant right away, like next month," Heather said, choking back a sob.

"They may want to wait, but let's ask the agency." Eric texted and they waited for an answer that came quickly. "They say not next month, but the month after."

"Maybe we should look for another surrogate, so we can do it sooner," Heather said through her tears.

"By the time that's all done, it'll probably be two months anyway."

"Ask the coordinator, Luka, what he thinks."

Eric texted Luka and his answer was almost word for word the same as Eric's. Why go through the whole vetting process again just to save a week or two. The other embryos were safely in Ukraine, so Eric and Heather tried to focus on work. Although different variants of Covid started to pop up, California did start opening up indoor venues with masks and social distancing still encouraged.

6

Spring 2021

SIX WEEKS LATER THE SECOND IMPLANTATION TOOK PLACE AND IT WAS A SUCCESS. Eric called his mother with the good news. "Wonderful!" she replied. "When's the due date?"

"February eighth."

"Aquarius. A good sign. Do you know if it's a girl or boy?"

"Girl. We knew before the implantation which embryos were male or female."

"My goodness!" Abby exclaimed. "And you had three! Are you planning on a second child this way too?"

Eric laughed. "Maybe if I win the lottery! Having three just meant that we could have more than one viable embryo to implant. Some people aren't that lucky, so if the first one didn't take like what happened to us, then they have no others. Some people take years just trying to get one embryo."

After calling her parents, Heather called Jed to tell him the news. "Fantastic, Heather. You and Eric must be so excited."

"I just hope this pandemic is over by then," she said. "Traveling will be a nightmare if they even let people travel."

"Oh it has to be over by then, don't you think?"

"I don't know. They understand so little about this virus."

"Hey, you have good news, Heather. No need to dwell on the bad stuff."

"Yeah, you're right," she sighed. "You always go out of your way to lift my spirits, Jed. I'll never forget the day we brought Chloe's ashes here. You promised us that you would watch over her and you always have." She stopped and swallowed hard. "And you've held my hand through all my visits. I feel like you're family."

"Thanks, Heather. By the way, I learned a new song for Chloe."

"Oh?" Heather smiled, blinking back a tear. "What is it?"

"The Garden Song." Jed sang a few notes. "You know, by Peter, Paul, and Mary."

"Who?"

"You never heard of Peter, Paul, and Mary?" Jed chuckled. "Boy, am I getting old. You know—'If I had a Hammer?' 'Leaving on a Jet Plane?' I've already been singing 'Puff the Magic Dragon' to her for quite some time."

"Oh, I know 'Puff the Magic Dragon.' I just didn't know who did it."

"They were very famous in the sixties."

Heather laughed. "Before my time."

"The first lines are 'Inch by inch, row by row, gonna make this garden grow' and then 'we are made of dreams and bones.' Very appropriate don't you think?"

"Oh yes. I'm sure Chloe loves hearing you sing all your songs, Jed." Heather gulped. "I'd better let you go. I'll be in touch." They hung up.

Heather went back to her computer, but instead of working she looked up the lyrics to "The Garden Song." Then she went to the Facebook group devoted to surrogacy. She liked reading the stories of the successes, and it didn't hurt to know that all the couples felt similar nervousness about the whole process.

Their surrogate, Iryna, had been texting over WhatsApp with them, so they got to know her and her two children. Hearing from her also helped make it all more real for Heather . . . more like she was family. She enjoyed the weekly photos of Iryna that the agency sent so she and Eric could track the pregnancy. Then she opened the photos on her computer to scroll through the many pictures she had of Chloe and shed a few tears.

The pandemic restrictions began to ease slightly after several weeks and Jed was able to open up the columbarium. Heather and Eric remained scrupulous, however, with mask wearing and social distancing to be ready to travel when the baby was born. Heather arrived at the columbarium one morning to find Jed singing to Chloe. Heather approached quietly and started joining in the chorus as she walked up next to him. Jed smiled at her and they finished the song together. "You learned the words to "The Garden Song?" Jed asked as he hugged her.

"Um hum," Heather beamed.

"How is everything going in Ukraine?" Jed asked as he wiped down the doors of the niches near Chloe's.

"It's pretty much a waiting game for now. We get reports with the vitals and ultrasounds of the baby. The surrogate is checked weekly for alcohol, tobacco and drug use. The agency visits are unannounced and they even check what's in her refrigerator to make sure she's eating healthily."

"They certainly are thorough. That's really good."

"And they take Iryna's picture so we can see how the pregnancy is progressing."

Jed smiled. "It's wonderful to see you so happy."

"It's been a long time."

He hugged her. "I know."

"I need to go, Jed. My in-laws are coming tonight for dinner. We haven't gotten together for months due to Covid. I've got to get to the store."

"Do they live here?"

"No. They live in Davis. It's only a bit more than an hour away, but we usually see them every couple of months." Heather left and Jed went back to work.

After she got home and put the groceries away, she looked over the design she had been working on and then sent it off. Eric worked part time at his office now that state and federal mandates had eased, so she was alone again in the house. She lay down to take a nap and woke after about half an hour from a disturbing dream that she had often. Even though she wasn't the one who was pregnant, as any expectant parent, she dreamt of all the issues that could arise during pregnancy and birth. Would the surrogate miscarry? Would she get preeclampsia and harm the baby? Would the baby have cerebral palsy or be deaf or blind? Would it have all its limbs? Heather tried to put all of that out of her mind as she started to get dinner ready.

Abby and Brian arrived about five, bitching about the bay area traffic. There was a time when Abby was more stoic about it, often making the drive from Davis to babysit and dote during Chloe's short life. Eric wasn't home yet, but Heather knew he too would complain about traffic. These were the moments Heather was pleased that she worked from home. "Should we keep our masks on?" Abby asked.

Heather frowned. "I think if we just sit six feet apart and don't hug we're okay." She got them their favorite cocktails and gingerly set them on the coffee table, her arms stretched out before her, and then retreated to a chair on the other side of the room.

"Thank you, dear," Abby smiled as she put the glass to her lips. "Ah—that's better."

"I wish all this pandemic crap was over," Brian said as he took a sip. He gazed over at Heather curled up in her chair in protective fashion. "You certainly don't need the added stress."

Heather managed to smile. "No, I don't. But it helps a little to hear someone acknowledge it."

Brian cocked his head and looked pleased that he had said the right thing. Abby took his hand and gave it a squeeze. A key grated in the lock and Eric burst into the room. Abby started to get up to give him a hug and then plopped back down onto the sofa in resignation. "Oh, Mom—I'm sorry." Eric peeled off his blazer and aimed an elbow greeting at Brian. Brian returned the salute half- heartedly. "Let me get out of these work clothes and I'll be right back."

Abby watched Eric retreat down the hall and then turned to Heather. "Eric has been sending us the pictures and charts that the representative from the agency sends you two about Iryna," Abby said. "Not much showing yet, but it's early. When will you go there?"

"I guess we'll go a few days before the due date, February eighth. The agency recommends not coming too early because we may have to stay awhile after."

"How long after?" Brian asked.

"There's a surrogate group on Facebook and some people say they have been able to leave after just two weeks, but others a lot longer."

"I guess it depends on the health of the baby," Abby mused.

"And Covid protocols in different countries," Eric interjected as he entered with his beer.

"Oh, this virus will be gone by then," Brian asserted.

"God, I hope so!" Heather sighed. "It will be overwhelming enough being in a foreign country in the middle of winter with a newborn!"

"We'll have had our second vaccinations by then," Eric said, settling down on the chair arm and putting his arm around Heather. "It'll be fine." She looked up at him and smiled.

"Have you chosen a name yet?" Abby asked.

"We're not sure," Eric answered quickly. He glanced down at Heather who nodded. "Well, we're thinking of Iryna, after the surrogate."

"Oh, that's sweet," Abby said, taking another sip.

"She spells it with a Y. We may make it I-R-I-N-A. We haven't decided for sure, though."

"Well, either way. It's a lovely name."

Heather smiled. "So do you two have any trips planned?"

"Not with this virus," Abby replied. "It's way too much trouble to fly anywhere. You have to be tested right before flying and possibly have to quarantine after you get to where you're going. Plus wearing a mask for all those hours in the airports and the plane also seems daunting. And if we drove, we wouldn't be able to eat inside restaurants or go inside most anywhere. It just wouldn't be a fun trip, always worrying about getting sick." Abby gasped and put down her drink. "Oh I'm sorry! You two will probably be facing this in February. Well, maybe Brian's right and Covid won't be so bad by the time you two go. After all, it is several months away."

"Well, one advantage of this pandemic is that we're getting a lot of work done around the house and yard," Brian added.

"That's great," piped Eric. "Making the best of being forced to stay home."

"And we're also getting back into our hobbies. Brian's dusted off his old easel." Abby grinned. "You should have seen his old shoe box full of dried out paint tubes."

"I hadn't realized how long it had been since I had painted. And your mother bought herself a new guitar."

Eric made a move toward his mother, but stopped himself. "That's wonderful," he said, sort of folding his arms around himself. "You've wanted to do music again for a while." He turned to Heather. "My mother was in a band, you know, back in the day."

"Wow. Like a rock and roll band?"

Abby nodded and smiled. "I was definitely a child of the sixties. But then children and career got in the way so I had to put it aside."

"Sorry Mom," Eric teased.

"It was worth it. Anyway, It's not like I ever thought I was going to be the next Bonnie Raitt!" she smiled.

Heather got up. "I need to check on dinner."

"Do you need help?" Abby asked.

"Nope. You're both so easy because you're vegetarians. I just have to make a salad. I bought some sourdough bread at the bakery and I made an easy butternut squash soup earlier today that's just simmering on the stove. It won't take me but a minute."

Heather went to the kitchen and Abby turned to Eric. "How is Heather doing?"

"Much better. She's starting to get excited about the new baby and not dwell on Chloe as much. But she's very worried, of course, that we might lose this child."

"As we all are, but we don't know that there was a genetic reason for Chloe's leukemia."

"It's not that she's anxious that we're carriers of some particular gene, just scared in general."

Abby nodded. "Every parent spends their lifetime worrying about their children. It goes with the territory."

"Dinner's ready!" Heather called from the kitchen.

7

Fall 2021

THE PANDEMIC ALTERNATELY EASED AND SURGED OVER THE NEXT SEVERAL MONTHS WHILE THE WEEKLY UPDATES ON IRYNA'S PREGNANCY SHOWED ALL WAS GOING WELL. Eric worked long hours to cover living expenses while they were in Ukraine, but fortunately costs were less than half of what they were accustomed to paying in San Francisco. Heather was pleasantly surprised to discover that their credit card points would cover most of their plane tickets.

Eric was still apprehensive about the whole thing. He had been calm and supportive to Heather when Chloe died. Heather had basically fallen apart to the point of having to be on a sedative, so Eric didn't have the luxury of facing his own grief at the time. It seemed to be happening now instead. At a time when he should be excited and elated, he was actually feeling a little sorry for himself. He wanted a child, but he felt conflicted, like he was somehow dishonoring Chloe. He couldn't talk about these feelings to Heather because she was happier than he'd seen her since before Chloe got sick. He would just have to bury his feelings . . . again. They had a subdued Christmas and New Years holiday, focusing more on plans for the trip and buying the latest baby items. Although they had saved some of Chloe's, there were always new contraptions and safety regulations to consider.

Some of Heather's friends had a baby shower for her in mid-January and that was when the unthinkable happened. The shower turned out to be a super-spreader event and Heather caught Covid. First she lost her taste and smell and then the fatigue and achiness set in. She parked herself in the bedroom and a double-masked Eric would leave her food on a tray outside the bedroom door.

Their plane was scheduled to leave on February 2nd and Heather was in no condition to fly, not that the airlines would let her. They had also been following the news of Russia sending ships, tanks and troops to Ukraine's borders. Iryna and the agency downplayed any fear that Russia would invade Ukraine. They kept telling Eric and Heather that the United States and the other NATO countries were sensationalizing. Things were fine in Ukraine and they shouldn't worry. Ukrainians were used to Russia trying to frighten them into submission.

Heather thought she would be able to fly as soon as she got better and tested negative, so she urged Eric to go alone. But as the day of departure got closer and closer, Heather got sicker and sicker. Her breathing became labored and the exhaustion was still overwhelming. "Mom?" Eric said when Abby answered her phone.

"Hi dear. How's Heather feeling?"

"Not so good. Mom . . . remember how we talked briefly about you possibly going with me to Ukraine?" Abby was quiet on the other end.

"Yes," she finally replied.

"I think I need you to come with me. Heather is still quite sick and probably won't test negative for a while. You wouldn't have to stay the whole time. Heather will join me as soon as she can."

"It's okay, Eric. I know you were trying to prep me for possibly going, but I just didn't think about it seriously." She paused for a moment. "I guess I have some planning to do. The flight is the second, right?"

"Yeah. It doesn't give you much time to prepare, I'm afraid."

"Well, my passport is current and I have a down jacket." She chuckled. "Those are the two most important things. It'll be fine."

"You need to get Covid insurance with a Ukrainian office and get a Covid test not more than one or two days before the plane leaves."

"Covid insurance? How do I do that?"

"I'll text or email you. Oh and what carrier do you use?"

"Carrier?"

"For your phone. Verizon? AT&T?"

"Uh, Verizon."

"Then you need to check with them about international rates and Internet access. Do you have WhatsApp on your phone?"

Abby sighed, hopefully not loud enough for Eric to hear. "No, but I've heard of it."

"It's a free way to talk to people around the world."

"Okay. I'll put the app on Brian's phone and mine. Anything else I need?"

"An international travel electrical adapter for charging your phone and computer and for anything else that you use."

"I guess just my hair dryer."

"I'm sorry, Mom."

"Don't be sorry. Anyway, it'll be nice to spend some one-on-one time with you, something we haven't done in many years." She paused, trying to think of other positive things to say. "And I'll be able to bond with my grandbaby at the beginning of her life."

"That's true."

"I do have some apprehensions about the threat of war. Putin is a scary person and he can't be trusted. I don't care what the Ukrainians are saying. War is on the horizon."

"Well, I don't wish it on the Ukrainians, of course," Eric replied, "but hopefully we'll be gone before anything happens."

"Hopefully," Abby sighed.

"I'd be more worried about Covid than anything. Seeing how it's affecting Heather . . ."

"Well, I'm vaccinated and pretty darn healthy for someone my age. Hey, the important thing is that we are picking up your baby." Abby took a deep breath. "I just can't let my apprehension about Russia and Putin get in the way."

"You're the best, Mom."

"You're not so bad yourself," she teased. They hung up. Abby wandered through the house and found Brian at his easel in the spare room. "Well, I guess I'm going to Ukraine."

Brian put down his brush. "I don't like that at all."

"There's no alternative. Eric needs me."

"I guess," he replied, staring at the canvas. "Why can't he go alone?"

"Two extra hands are always handy when dealing with a baby." Brian said nothing. "Hey," she said, poking him. "Think of all the peace and quiet you'll have here. I won't be disturbing you while you're painting."

Brian ran his hand over the spot she poked and glared at her. "It's a terrible time to travel with Covid and now Ukraine on the verge of war."

"What do you suggest? Leave the baby there?"

"The situation is not that black and white."

Abby frowned. "Okay, let's frame this differently. It's a trip to a country I probably would never go to otherwise. And it'll be an adventure. To tell you the truth, I'm more concerned about the damn weather! You know how much I hate the cold!"

"Reframing doesn't improve a bad painting," he said, screwing a cap back onto a tube of paint. "But you've made up your mind. I'll be here, warm and worrying."

"Fine." Abby sniffed. Silence fell between them. "Well, I have some things to do and think about." She went into her office to find her passport and make phone calls to cancel appointments she had. Then she went to her closet to find whatever cold weather clothes she had.

"How did your mother react?" Heather asked Eric through the bedroom door.

"Surprised, but okay."

"You had mentioned it as a possibility, hadn't you?"

"I guess she hadn't thought it would actually happen."

"I'm still hoping I can come in a week or so."

"A week? Come on, Heather!"

"Okay. Maybe a couple of weeks."

Eric decided not to reply, but he knew it would be longer than that . . . if at all. Anyway, he was hoping they'd be home after a couple of weeks. Some of the people on that Facebook page said they were able to go home two weeks after the birth, but they weren't picking up their babies during a pandemic and most of them were from European countries. Their plane rides home were significantly shorter, of course. And the agency had already warned them that the embassy was taking longer to process passports and U.S. birth certificates because of Covid.

Meanwhile Abby was a flurry of activity with less than a week to prepare for the trip. She sent out emails to the people who needed to know. She called Paige who reacted similarly to Brian. She packed and repacked trying to take as little as possible, because she knew Eric would have stuff for the baby as well as himself.

Heather shouted directions and guidance through the bedroom door about what Eric needed to pack for the baby. "I have the list you texted me!" he shouted back, getting a bit irritated.

"The car seat is for the plane. The rest of the stuff you rent. I'll take care of that with Luka at the agency. I'll get a bassinet and a stroller. Do you think you'll need a changing table?"

"Heather! Stop worrying about it. We can do all that once we're there. You just take care of the embassy. Let them know only one parent is coming and what we need to do because of that."

"At least they're skipping the DNA tests because of Covid. That would have been a major problem since I wouldn't be there."

Eric sighed. "I've got it covered! But I'm also worried about you being alone and so sick."

"A bunch of people have offered to fix me meals and leave them outside the door. They want to help anyway so this makes them feel like they're doing something. At least I won't have to worry about giving you Covid, so I can roam around the house instead of staying confined to these four walls. Did you tell your mom about doing a Covid test within forty-eight hours of leaving and it has to be a PCR test, not a home one?"

"Yes. I told her," Eric groaned.

"What will we do if it's positive for either one of you?" Heather asked.

"Let's not go there please. I feel fine!"

"But some people don't have symptoms and still have it."

"Heather!" Eric bellowed. "There's enough to worry about without adding something that we don't even know is a problem!"

Heather was silent for a few minutes. "I'm sorry. I just—"

"This is stressful for both of us," Eric sighed. "The answer to your question is that we will figure out something. Okay? Let's wait and see the results of the test and then we'll talk about it.

I've got to go. I have other last minute things to do."

The next day Eric tried to keep his stress level low and his annoyance under check. He kept telling himself that Heather was not only dealing with the mental nervousness, but she was physically sick as well. He had to admit that he had no idea what to do if he tested positive. He couldn't send Abby alone. Not just because it would be too much for his mother to handle alone, but the hospital would never give the baby to someone who wasn't a parent.

It was finally time to be tested. He went to the testing site early. "When will you have the results?" he asked.

"When is your flight?" the tester responded.

"Two days."

"You should have it by then."

"Should? I have to have it by then!"

"I understand, sir."

Eric sighed and left, feeling even more stressed. He called the testing site several times the next day, trying to get his results. Finally that evening

the call came through and he could breathe a sigh
of relief.

8

February 2022

THE DAY OF DEPARTURE FINALLY ARRIVED. Brian drove Abby to Eric and Heather's house and then took Abby and Eric to the airport. Heather shed many tears through the door as they said their goodbyes. Eric was laden down with luggage: the car seat, a large suitcase full of baby items and his own backpack. Abby just had her purse and one small suitcase. They must have looked pretty silly in their heavy jackets and boots in sunny California, but they had no choice. They would have needed another suitcase just for those items if they didn't wear them.

Eric and Abby were finally seated in the plane for the first leg of the arduous journey. They would fly from San Francisco to Houston where the layover was two hours, and then board a flight for Istanbul. They had some N95 masks for the airports and flights. The N95 masks were harder to come by for people who weren't healthcare workers, but Abby had a friend who had stockpiled a few. The anxiety over what Russia was doing in Ukraine overshadowed everything, as well.

"What a time to be traveling," Eric groaned as he stretched his legs out during takeoff.

"We can only hope Iryna and the Ukrainians on the news are right," Abby replied. "It's hard to believe they aren't scared of what Putin is doing."

"Maybe they're right. It wouldn't be the first time the news stations made a big deal out of something that might not be such a big deal."

"I guess I have more faith in journalists than you do," she teased.

"Ha, ha, Mom."

"Do you ever wish you were still in the newspaper business?"

"Sure. But there's not much newspaper business to be part of anymore."

"But you enjoyed it."

"It was fun . . . a great job . . . but not very lucrative."

"True. You've been good at every job you've had."

"Well thanks, Mom."

"You and Paige are my pride and joy," Abby smiled at her son.

The plane landed in Istanbul twelve hours later. It was a challenge wearing the masks for all that time, especially trying to sleep. The airlines hadn't been serving meals on domestic flights since Covid began, but Turkish Airlines had to give the passengers something since the flight was so long. Abby made for quite a challenge, being a vegetarian and not a fan of hot and spicy food. The flight attendant tried to accommodate as best she could, but there wasn't much available to pick from. Eric ate both his and Abby's meals, praising the food, while Abby nibbled on fruit and vegetables and lots of bread.

There was only supposed to be a one-hour layover in Istanbul, so their first introduction to Turkey was one filled with angst. A Turkish- speaking woman in a uniform was standing at the gate yelling in Turkish. "What's she saying?" Abby asked.

"I'm not sure," Eric replied. "A couple of young guys are headed toward her so I guess she's looking for them."

Then they heard her say "Kyiv" and realized she was probably looking for passengers going to Kyiv. They walked over to the woman. "Kyiv?" she asked.

"Yes," Eric answered. "We're going to Kyiv."

"Come!" she waved as she took off walking at such a fast clip, Abby and Eric had to run to keep up.

She led them running through the airport. Abby tripped getting off one of the walkways and landed on her knees. "Dammit!"

"Mom!" Eric came running back to her. "Are you alright?"

Abby got up slowly. "Yes, thank goodness!"

The woman approached them. "Okay?" she asked.

Abby nodded wearily. The woman then took off jogging back to the two young guys. "Go ahead,

Eric. You run with them. I'm walking. Just ask them to hold the damn plane until I get there."

Eric started walking fast, turning around every couple of minutes to check on Abby. She waved him off as she limped along. When Abby got to the gate for the flight to Kyiv, she noticed Eric and the two young men who had run across the airport with them. They were sitting on chairs looking angry. "The plane's been delayed," Eric scoffed.

"You're not serious!" Abby gasped, dropping onto the chair next to Eric. "We ran all the way here for nothing?"

"Apparently."

"Did they say how long?"

"No."

"Where's the wicked witch of the west?" she asked, rubbing her knees.

Eric laughed. "She left to go hassle somebody else I guess."

A couple of hours went by. Eric was reading a friend's manuscript that he had promised to edit while Abby fidgeted, went to the restroom, and read on her Kindle. She glanced often at the arrival and departure board, and basically fretted. "This mask-wearing all these hours is getting old really fast!" she finally said, tugging at the straps.

Eric shrugged. "Not much we can do about it."

"I haven't minded it up til now. At home it's just an hour or so at the most. But we've had these on for how many hours?"

"I don't know." He looked at his watch. "Eighteen or so? But the good news is that the flight from Istanbul to Kyiv is short . . . less than two hours."

Finally someone came on the loudspeaker, but of course spoke in Turkish. Abby looked around at the other passengers waiting to board their flight and listened to the groans. "Uh oh," she said and just then the English translation came over the loudspeaker.

"Flight number 216 has been cancelled. There are no more flights this evening for Kyiv. We have automatically put you on a morning flight at nine am. If this is not satisfactory, please go speak to a ticket agent."

"Oh no," Eric sighed. "I guess we need to find a hotel."

"Aren't they supposed to set us up in a hotel if a flight is cancelled?" Abby asked.

"I think it's all different now with Covid. You stay here and watch the luggage. I'll go find out." Eric went to the desk and stood in line for what seemed to Abby like an eternity. He finally came back. "Well . . . you're not going to be happy."

"What? There are no hotel rooms left?" she asked.

"It's not that. They won't let us leave the airport due to Covid."

Abby's jaw dropped. "We have to sleep in the airport?"

"Looks that way."

"And we have to wear these damn masks for another twenty-four hours?"

"Yep. And . . ." Eric paused and inhaled. "There are no restaurants open because of the pandemic. There's just whatever snacks you can find at that duty-free shop over there." He pointed to a store with an open door.

"They have food? It looks just like liquor."

"That's why I said snacks."

"Well, at this point, maybe I'll just forget snacking and go along with a good, stiff drink."

"Come on Mom. Try to make the best of it. It's an adventure!"

"Yes, I recall telling myself that." Abby glanced around the airport. "We need to find ourselves a comfortable place to park for the night, far away from people. That way we can at least take our masks off for a breather. I guess we have to wear them to sleep."

"Probably a good idea," Eric sighed. "But you're right. Let's find ourselves some nice chairs. Let's get away from here where the duty-free shop and the gates are." They got up and walked through the airport until they found rows of empty chairs at a gate that wasn't in use. "How about here?" he said. "There are restrooms nearby and we can bring our snacks and drinks."

"Okay, but this time you stay with our stuff and I'll find us something at the duty-free shop," Abby said. "I need to walk a bit."

Eric agreed and Abby walked back to the store. She returned with beer, peanuts and chips. "So even in Istanbul you can find Doritos and Planters!" Eric chuckled.

"I did buy Turkish beer though."

"Efes Pilsen," Eric read off the label. He took a sip. "Mm. It's good. You'll like it, I think."

Abby took a sip. "Yeah, it is good. I guess I can say I had something Turkish since I couldn't eat the food on the airplane." She took a handful of peanuts. "I just may lose weight on this trip. I don't think either Turkey or Ukraine is big on vegetarianism. Their food seems quite meat-oriented."

"You'll find food in Kyiv I'm sure. It's a huge city with almost three million people."

Abby nodded. "I'm sure everything will be fine once we get there. And anyway, we won't have time to eat once we have the baby. I remember when you were a newborn. As soon as you would fall asleep, I would have to decide which was more important: eating or sleeping." She laughed. "I usually chose sleep."

"But there will be two of us there all the time. Dad had to go to work so it was just you all day long."

"That's true." They sat quietly sipping and snacking . . . each lost in their thoughts. "I guess I'll call Brian on that WhatsApp thing. What time is it in California?"

"Late morning."

"I hope he can figure out how to answer the phone on that app."

"It's not difficult."

"For him, everything having to do with his phone is difficult." She dialed but he didn't pick up. "I told you." Her phone rang shortly after that. "Okay, it's Brian. I take it back. He figured it out." Eric got up and went to another set of chairs to call Heather and Luka to tell them about the newest snag.

When Eric took out his friend's book again, Abby decided to go for another walk in the airport before settling into her chair for the night. A television glowed in one of the empty lounge areas and she stopped to watch a Turkish news channel. Although she couldn't understand what was being said, she did notice the pictures of Russian tanks and a map of Ukraine showing where these tanks were on the northern and eastern edges. She couldn't understand why Iryna and the Ukrainians were not worried about this, but it was more reassuring to believe them than to worry that they were wrong.

9

ERIC AND ABBY SLEPT FITFULLY, ALTERNATING BETWEEN CURLED UP OR SPRAWLED OVER THE VINYL WAITING ROOM CHAIRS. They woke up starving, but a long walk and eventually a familiar scent led them to an open kiosk with coffee and pastries. Their plane was scheduled to take off at nine, but didn't actually leave until noon. "Do you think all this is due to the Russian troops on Ukraine's borders?" Abby asked Eric as the plane finally taxied and lifted off.

Eric looked over at her wearily. "I think this happens enough without the threat of war or a pandemic."

"Yeah, but . . . oh never mind. I just wish I wasn't so exhausted and could be enthusiastic about traveling to a new country."

"Just keep your eyes on the prize, Mom."

"Yeah. Baby Irina." She squeezed his hand.

"Uh—I forgot to tell you." Abby's grip on his hand loosened. "We've decided to make Irina her middle name and Jillian her first name."

Abby rocked her head, letting the new name settle in. "Beautiful," she finally said, squeezing his hand again. "Jillian Irina. Abby looked out the window for a few minutes. "Is someone from the agency picking us up at the airport?"

"Yes, they arranged for a driver."

"And the apartment, right?"

"Yeah. Luka from the agency took care of everything—even delivery of the bassinet and stroller as soon as the baby is born. I just sent him money."

Eric took out his friend's novel, so Abby turned to look out the window. Then she tried her Kindle, but found it hard to concentrate. She thought about what she had seen on the television. Was Russia going to invade Ukraine while they were there? They were going to be staying in Kyiv, the capital. One would assume that's where Russia would go first. But all the Ukrainians continued to deny that. They should know—right? She tried to bury those thoughts.

They were not serving any purpose. She had enough to worry about. Eric finally put the manuscript away. "Did you finish it?" she asked.

"Yeah. I had hoped to finish it before the baby came."

"The baby might be due in a few days, but you never know," Abby replied. "We could be waiting for awhile or not at all. You were ten days early."

"Iryna said her two kids were born right on their due dates, so I'm thinking that will be the case now too. But if not, we'll be able to do some sightseeing. Eric smiled. "Or we'll be taking care of a baby immediately!"

"My weather app says it is fifteen degrees," she said as she glanced at her phone. "And it's not like we have the luxury of spending too much time inside buildings due to Covid. But I'm sure there's some stuff to see. Have you researched any places to visit in Kyiv?"

"Not really. We can when we get there and see where our apartment is."

"Do you have the address?"

"In an email, but I can't access it on the plane."

"I guess there's a part of me that isn't believing all this is happening," Abby said, pulling on her mask. "I can't wait to take this thing off! I don't know how doctors and nurses do it!"

"They just get used to it. I've gotten pretty used to wearing a mask by now."

The pilot came on the loudspeaker. "We are starting our descent. Please stay seated and fasten your seatbelts."

"Glad he translated into English, although it is kind of obvious that we are landing soon," Abby remarked.

Eric exhaled sharply. "We got here. I wasn't so sure we would."

"I know what you mean. So—?" Abby asked tentatively. "Do you also think they are going to invade Ukraine?"

Eric looked into Abby's eyes. "Come on, Mom. You know they are."

"Are we going to be able to get the baby?"

"Yeah. I mean, sure. It'll work out," Eric backpedaled.

"I hope so," Abby sighed. Her mind started going in many different directions. Was Eric just trying to gloss over what he's truly thinking for her sake? She didn't want to believe that they might not be able to take Jillian home . . . or that they were going to find themselves in the middle of a war zone. She would make herself believe that Eric was right. She couldn't let herself think any other way.

The plane landed. They found a man at the baggage claim holding a sign that said "Eric Stover." Eric and Abby approached the man. "I'm Eric Stover. Do you speak English?"

"I wait for your bags," he replied.

Eric smiled and nodded, then turned to Abby. "You wait here with our carry-ons and I'll get our bags," he pointed to a chair and set down his backpack. Abby sat on the chair, but the driver stayed standing where he was.

They followed the driver to his car and were soon on their way. Abby stared out the window at the tall buildings as they entered Kyiv. They could be in San Francisco, New York, London . . . the main difference was the gold domed tops and the statues everywhere.

They arrived at the apartment the agency had rented for them. It was actually quite spacious with a large living room and good-sized bedroom. The kitchen was wide enough for a table and chairs to fit in. The bathroom was interesting with a circular door that surrounded a tiny shower. "We're going to have a hard time soaping ourselves in this shower!" Abby laughed.

"Better than a tiny bathtub I guess," said Eric as he opened the door to look inside.

"Do we know where the closest grocery store is?" Abby asked after they both had showered and unpacked.

"I'll look." Eric found one on his map app a few blocks away. "It looks like we are in a great part of the city. It's downtown, I guess. Lots of stores and restaurants are nearby and we are close to a park and museums."

"That's great. Now if the temperature would at least go up twenty degrees so I could stand to be outside . . ." Abby shook her head.

"I know. Well, bundle up because we have to buy some groceries."

Abby put on a sweatshirt, a down vest and a down jacket over all of that. She put on a knit facemask and two pairs of gloves. "What do you think? Think I'll be warm enough?"

Eric shook his head and scoffed. "You look ridiculous, but yes, I think you'll be warm enough."

"I brought my hiking boots because they have the best soles. I don't want to slip on the ice."

Eric laughed. "Mom, you grew up on the East Coast—don't you think you're being a little dramatic?"

"Not at my age."

Eric shrugged. "Are you ready to brave the elements?"

"Very funny!" They went outside, walked a few blocks and found themselves in a huge underground shopping center. "This is like Minneapolis."

"What do you mean?" Eric asked.

"Because of the cold, I guess, downtown Minneapolis has a huge shopping area downtown that's elevated and enclosed rather than underground. It covers a lot of blocks."

"Then I guess we're lucky that Luka found us this apartment near downtown."

They each took a basket and separated to look for food they each wanted. Abby was surprised to see all the fresh fruits and vegetables. She had thought that a place this cold would have a limited supply, but apparently they imported a good variety. She filled her basket, having no idea what anything cost since everything was written in Ukrainian. Eric had said that things were much cheaper here, so she wasn't concerned.

Finding crackers, bread, cheese and nuts, however, was a different story and those were her staple foods. There were very few boxes of crackers and bags of nuts and they all seemed to be different than anything familiar to her. When she got to the bread aisle, she saw very little that looked appealing. Good bread had been what she had been looking forward to and she was quite surprised that it all looked like Wonder Bread.

But even worse was the cheese. Everything was in Ukrainian and she had no idea what kind of cheese she was looking at. The packaging was so different; it all looked like butter to her. She did see a package of Philadelphia Cream Cheese so she bought that. At least she would know what she was eating, even if it wasn't exactly the healthiest cheese she could buy. She went back to the crackers aisle, hoping something familiar like that would appear. The only thing familiar was a package of Oreo cookies, not exactly what one normally eats spread with cream cheese.

"Did you find anything you like?" Eric said, his basket filled with meat and fish and familiar deli products.

"Lots of fruits and vegetables and cream cheese," she said. "Nothing's in English and I don't know what I'm buying."

"Did you see any bagels for the cream cheese? There's probably smoked salmon somewhere."

"The bread selection is paltry."

Eric shrugged. "So what are you going to do?"

"I guess lose weight while I'm here," Abby laughed. "Well, we did pass that croissant bakery on the way here. I can eat one of those for breakfast with my cream cheese. I'll manage. Don't worry."

"Did you ask anyone for help reading the labels?"

"No. Let's just look around. Maybe there are other stores that sell stuff I like. I'm sorry I'm such a picky eater. It's just hard with restaurants closed due to Covid. I'm sure there are good restaurants here."

"Well, we can get take-out at least."

"I'll be fine. We didn't come to Ukraine to eat and drink." She smiled. "We came to welcome baby Jillian into the world."

They took their baskets to check out and Abby started to put the bags of fruit and vegetables on the counter. The clerk looked at her quizzically. Eric looked around the store, trying to understand why she didn't just ring up the produce. "Is there something wrong?" He finally said to the clerk who continued to stare at them both. "Do you speak English?"

The clerk sighed and grabbed the bags. Abby stayed at the counter while Eric followed the clerk back to the produce section. He watched as she weighed and tagged each bag. Then she brought them back to the check out counter. "What did she do?" Abby asked.

Eric shook his head and smiled. "There were labels and pictures on each section. We were supposed to do it ourselves. And it didn't even matter whether we spoke Ukrainian. It was easy and we could have done it ourselves."

Abby laughed. "Oh well, we learn as we go."

10

ABBY AND ERIC SPENT MOST OF THE REST OF THE DAY ON THEIR PHONES AND COMPUTERS TELLING EVERYONE ABOUT THEIR NIGHT IN THE ISTANBUL AIRPORT. The apartment only had one bedroom and a sofa in the living room. Although the couch was comfortable, it meant they would take turns sleeping. When the baby would arrive, however, sleep would be a rare commodity anyway. The bassinet and stroller were accounted for, and they both agreed that the desk in the living room could serve perfectly well as a changing table.

"I'll sleep on the sofa tonight," Abby said. "I never sleep well anyway so I might as well be out here. Insomnia is just part of this damn aging process."

"But will you be comfortable?" Eric asked.

"As comfortable as one can be wide awake," Abby sniffed. "I'll be fine."

"Goodnight, Mom."

Eric was still sleeping when Abby woke up from a brief snooze. She went to the kitchen for her customary cup of tea and remembered she hadn't bought any milk to put in it. She couldn't figure out if there was any nonfat milk at the store and she didn't like it without milk. "Oh well, I don't really need to drink tea," she thought. She showered and sat down with a crossword puzzle book to wait for Eric to get up. They had planned to explore the neighborhood and do a bit of sightseeing. A newborn baby would not be able to go out in this cold, so they wanted to explore as much as they could until the birth.

There was a television at the apartment, but it seemed futile to try and figure out how to use it since everything would be in Ukrainian anyway. She took out her computer to check the news. Russia continued to up the ante on Ukraine's borders. It made her very uneasy, but everyone in Kyiv seemed to be going about their business as usual. Kyiv was pretty far from the northern and eastern borders, but she found it hard to accept that there wouldn't be some sort of attack on the capital city.

"Good morning," Eric said as he crossed through the living room to get to the bathroom.

Abby waved at her laptop. "Shouldn't we be concerned about what Russia is doing? I know what Luka and even Zelensky are saying but . . ."

Eric stopped and sighed. "I doubt Zelensky, as president of Ukraine, would tell people not to worry if it wasn't true."

Abby shrugged. "I hope you're right, but why else is Putin doing this?"

"We have a lot to worry about as it is, Mom. Let's go with what Zelensky says. It's easier that way. I'm going to take a shower. Have you had breakfast?"

"I thought I'd check out that croissant bakery when we go out."

"Okay. I'll be ready in a few minutes."

"No hurry. The later we go, the warmer it will be."

"Mom, are you going to continually complain about the cold?"

"No, Eric," Abby replied, pursing her lips. "But at least let me get used to it. A lot of years have passed since I've been in ten-degree weather. And by the way, it is snowing right now."

"Luka says it basically snows all day, every day, but lightly."

"Ugh. Now I have to worry about falling on the ice."

"I'm sure they clear the sidewalks," Eric said irritably as he left for the bathroom.

Abby bundled up with layers while Eric appeared in sneakers and a sweatshirt. Abby picked at the knit fabric. "Even when you were a kid back in Massachusetts, you never wore a warm jacket."

"Yeah, yeah," Eric growled, brushing her hand away.

They picked up some croissants at the bakery and ate them as they walked around. The apartment was close to some incredible buildings and churches, so there was much to marvel at. The gold-topped domes and the intricate architecture had them both in awe. There were many interesting statues placed on almost every street and there were fascinating murals depicting the war in 2014. "I wish Heather could see these," Eric said as he stood in front of a wall done by a local street artist.

"What was that war about?" Abby asked.

"I think it was about protesting." Eric scrolled through his phone. "Here it is. It was called the Revolution of Dignity or Maidan Revolution."

"Is that when they successfully removed the pro-Russian president?"

Eric read a little more off his phone. "Yeah. I guess what's happening now is a direct result of that."

"When was Zelensky elected?" Abby asked.

"2019," Eric replied. He studied his phone for a moment. "Poroshenko was president starting in 2014 and helped push back Russian influence and got Ukraine into democracy, but there were accusations of corruption."

"Just another billionaire oligarch in the end, I guess," Abby scoffed. "Even if he did good things for Ukraine."

"Come on, Mom. You of all people know how politics works."

Abby nodded. "Well, this Zelensky guy seems okay even though he's had no political experience." She laughed. "Although he did play a president on television."

"Yeah. I heard that. He seems to be liked, although we'll have to see how he handles this thing going on with Russia." He took hold of Abby's arm. "Let's venture down into that huge shopping center underground and warm up."

"And stay away from falling bombs."

"Mom! Let's focus on why we're here." He pulled her toward the hill they would need to walk down.

They spent a couple of hours wandering around the shops. "I guess we haven't any room for souvenirs," Abby said as she looked at some of the dolls.

"We could fit small stuff if you really want to get something."

"Nah. It's okay." She smiled. "At my age I'm trying to get rid of stuff, not add more."

They bought a few more grocery items and hiked up the hill to the apartment. Eric got on his computer to do some work, figuring he wouldn't have much time once Jillian arrived. Abby got on her computer as well, and opened Microsoft Word. She stared at the screen and let her mind wander in many directions, remembering how much she enjoyed writing. She Googled a bit and found a site with ideas on how to spark your creative writing juices and decided to try some of them as a way to begin.

The first exercise was to write a two thousand five hundred-word autobiography. Okay. She felt confident enough to do that. She started writing and the words poured out. When she paused to check her word count, she was shocked to see that she had written seven thousand words and she felt like she had barely scratched the surface. She was enjoying the process and the hours flew by. Eric eventually interrupted her thoughts. "I'm going to that restaurant around the corner and get some take-out for dinner. I want to try some Ukrainian food. How about you?"

"You know me," she said, glancing up from the screen. "I probably won't like it."

"Do you want to come and see what they have? They probably have something you'll like. Potato pancakes? Borscht? Dumplings? There's a lot that isn't made with meat."

"Okay," Abby replied distractedly, once again typing. Just bring me something you think I'll like." Abby continued writing until Eric returned with a large bag.

"I brought a bunch of stuff. If you don't like any of it, I'll have plenty to eat for a couple of days," he grinned.

They sat down at the table and took out the paper plates and plastic forks that had come with the food. "It's good, but kind of greasy," she said.

"Yeah. That's what makes it good."

"To you!" she laughed.

"Tonight you can have the bed," Eric said as they finished cleaning up and he went back on his computer.

""'I'm fine on the couch," she responded. "It's quite comfortable. But I will go into the bedroom to call Brian. It's about ten in the morning there, right?"

"Yeah. I'll call Heather when I'm done with this, right before I go to bed."

Abby went into the bedroom and called Brian. "The news in the U.S. is very grim about how Russia is gearing up for an invasion," Brian said.

"I know, but it's totally different here. Everyone acts like nothing is happening. I don't know what to think. Eric wants to ignore it." She sighed. "Well, Eric is right about one thing. There isn't a thing we can do about it." They talked for a few more minutes and Abby brought up her autobiography. "It was a small exercise and suddenly I had something like a manuscript."

"Would you consider publishing it?" Brian asked.

"No!" Abby answered emphatically. "My life's not that interesting."

"I wouldn't say that, but it will be even more interesting once you can add the story of picking up your grandbaby in Ukraine. Especially with all the recent developments."

"Hmm. Maybe so. I'll think about it." They hung up and then she and Eric changed places. She took out the sheets and made up the sofa while Eric took his computer and phone and went into the bedroom.

11

February 6, 2022

"MOM! MOM!" ERIC EXCLAIMED AS HE SHOOK ABBY'S SHOULDER. "She's coming!"

Abby groaned and rolled over. "Who's coming?" she mumbled.

"The baby! I just got a text!"

"Oh—" Then it finally sunk in. "OH!" Abby scrambled out of bed. "What time is it?"

"Three a.m."

"Okay," she replied, stumbling toward the bathroom. "I'll be ready in a sec!"

"Why don't you wake up with a quick shower?" Eric suggested. "Remember we have to stay in the hospital for two nights, even if she's healthy and all goes well. I'll pack up some food and the baby items we'll need to take with us."

"Do we have time for all that?"

"Iryna just arrived at the hospital and we can't actually be in the room with her while she's giving birth."

"Did she call?" Abby asked.

"No, Luka did. But it'll be a little while."

"You're packing food? Won't they feed us some terrible cafeteria hospital food?"

"I don't know. But it probably won't be food you'll eat anyway." Eric winked and grinned. When she came out of the bathroom Eric said, "Luka just texted again. We have to get tested before going to the hospital."

"How are we going to do that?"

"Apparently they'll come right here."

"But how long will that take?"

"Luka said they'd come right away." The bell rang while Abby was in the bedroom getting dressed and Eric opened the door. Two people stood there in HAZMAT suits, but said nothing. "Oh," Eric said. Since they did not move, he started waving them in. "Come in." The two entered and stood silently in the living room. "Do you speak English?"

One of the people said, "a little" and then it became clear that it was a woman.

Abby came out of the bedroom and stopped in her tracks, her eyes wide with surprise at the way they were dressed. She then looked over at Eric, who urged her to come over—then pointing to their noses. "When will you have the results?" he asked the woman as she opened her bag and took out a test kit. She held up two fingers. "Two days?" Eric moaned.

"Hours," she replied.

Eric breathed a sigh of relief. "How will we get the results?" She took out her phone and pointed to it. "You need my number?"

She nodded and said, "text."

The other HAZMAT wearer swabbed Abby and Eric's noses and packed up his stuff. "We need to get to the hospital so please text us as soon as you get the results," Eric said as he let them out the front door. The woman nodded, but he wasn't sure she fully understood him.

Luka texted Eric that Iryna was dilated ten centimeters and delivery had begun. "I wonder if we can start the trip to the hospital before we get the results," Abby pondered. "I mean we both feel fine. I'm sure we're negative."

"Probably best to wait," Eric replied. "Even if only one of us tests positive, it'll certainly change how this will play out."

"I guess you're right," Abby sighed. "Well, if we're both negative, where do we go when we get to the hospital if we can't go to the delivery room?"

"I don't know. I guess we wait in the waiting room."

"I just hope they speak more English in the hospital than they did in the grocery store," Abby groaned.

Eric gave her a sideways look. "You are in a foreign country, Mom."

"I just thought people in other countries learned English in school and that more people would speak it."

Eric shook his head. "Maybe that's true in France or Italy or Japan, but probably not here. Just use that Google Translator App."

"What?"

"I thought I told you to put it on your phone," Eric replied irritably.

"Maybe you did." She took out her phone and started scrolling. "I'll get it now."

They both sat anxiously playing with their phones, waiting for the text from the Covid testers. "Oh man! I forgot. We have to bring our own sheets to the hospital."

"Seriously?"

"That's what Luka had said." He got up and found a couple of sheets in the bedroom closet.

"What about blankets?"

"I don't know. He only said sheets. Bringing blankets would be a pain anyway."

Eric's phone pinged. "Both negative!" He got them an Uber immediately.

They arrived at the hospital and entered the admitting area. Eric went up to the window and asked if Iryna had given birth yet. The two women sitting at the desk did not smile and looked at him blankly. He took out his phone and used the app, expecting a smile with their reply. Instead one of them answered with one word. "Sit!" she said pointing across the room.

"Well?" Abby said when Eric sat down next to her.

"Not yet, I guess."

"You guess?"

"One thing I've noticed here in Ukraine. People don't smile much and don't use many words."

"Maybe it's because we're using a surrogate and they frown on that," Abby scoffed. "A lot of people think the surrogates are being coerced and—"

"Mom. They are just not smiling. Don't read anything into it. It's probably just that they don't speak English."

"Maybe they're starting to worry about a Russian invasion after all," she replied. "Have you texted Heather?"

"Of course!"

"How's she feeling?"

"Not great, but not as horrible as she felt when we were home."

"I should let Brian and Paige know." She took out her phone and started to text.

"I'll text Paige," Eric said. "She's been texting me a lot . . . she's very excited about being an aunt again."

"I know. She and Chloe were so close."

They waited about half an hour until one of the women behind the glass partition called out. "Come!"

Eric and Abby stood obediently and followed the woman through a door, up some stairs and down a hall. They figured they were being brought to the room they were going to be staying in after Jillian was born. They were hoping they could leave their suitcase and backpack before venturing into wherever the baby would be. But instead they were brought into the room where Iryna was lying on a bed and Jillian was in a bassinet next to her. 'Oh my God!" Abby and Eric both exclaimed, rushing to the bassinet.

"She's beautiful," Iryna said.

Eric stroked Jillian's cheek and said, "Thank you so much, Iryna. She is."

Abby wiped away her tears of joy and took Iryna's hand. "You look incredible for just having given birth!"

Iryna smiled. "I am tired." The doctor came into the room and said something in Ukrainian "He says she is very healthy," Iryna translated.

"Why is she still hooked up to machines?" Abby asked.

"It's normal here in Ukraine," Iryna answered. She then spoke to the doctor. "He says he will get the nurse to unhook her and you can hold her."

The doctor left and Luka arrived with a shopping bag. "Congratulations!"

"Thanks Luka," Eric said. "This is my mother, Abby."

"Nice to meet you," Abby and Luka replied in unison.

"Delivery went very well, I understand." Luka said to Iryna. "Quick and easy."

"Yes," Iryna answered. "No problems."

Luka turned to Eric. "Have they shown you the room you'll be staying in until you can take her home?"

"Not yet. They brought us straight here."

"Well, here are some gifts for you." Luka handed over the shopping bag.

"Thanks, Luka," Eric said as he took the bag.

"I just wanted to check in. I'll text you later."

Luka left just as the nurse arrived to unhook Jillian from the machines. She picked her up looked from Eric to Abby and back again, wondering who she should hand the baby to. Iryna said something in Ukrainian and the nurse placed Jillian into Eric's arms. "Oh my sweet baby!" Eric gushed as he gazed into Jillian's arms.

"Let me get a picture to send Heather, Brian and Paige," Abby said, taking her phone out of her purse.

They took the photos and then the nurse said something to Iryna. "She said she needs to examine me and she will meet you in your room with the baby."

"No one has shown us where the room is," Eric said.

Iryna spoke to the nurse and then said, "She will get someone to show you."

"How long were you in labor?" Abby asked.

"Not long. Few hours. It wasn't bad."

"Lucky you! This man took forever to come out of me! Thirty-six hours!"

"Oh that must have been awful!"

"Eric just didn't want to leave that warm, cozy womb!" Iryna laughed and then yawned. "Oh you need to sleep," Abby added.

"It's okay. The doctor needs to examine me. Then I sleep."

The nurse returned with another woman who said, "Come." Eric handed Jillian to the nurse and he and Abby followed the other woman down the hall and up some stairs to the room that was to be their home with Jillian for the next two nights.

12

THE ROOM THEY WERE BROUGHT TO WAS MORE LIKE A FORGOTTEN WAITING ROOM THAN A PLACE TO CARE FOR A NEWBORN. There was a padded vinyl bench like one would find in an airport, a vinyl lounge chair and ottoman, a bassinet, a changing table and nothing else. "Maybe that door—" Abby said half aloud, but when Eric swung it wide open, it only led into a tiny bathroom. They glanced back around them, and then at one another, their eyebrows slowly rising. "Well," Abby shrugged, "I'll take the chair."

"Are you sure?"

Abby gave him a look. "You really think you are going to sleep on that chair and ottoman?"

"I can sleep anywhere," Eric replied, sticking his chin out. "You're the one with insomnia."

"I don't think either of us is going to get a whole lot of sleep the next two nights." She laughed. "Make that the next two years for you!"

Eric grinned at her. "How well I remember."

"Should we put the sheets on these so-called beds now?"

"Anything to keep the cold vinyl from sticking to us."

"That's what I was thinking. Do you see any blankets?" Abby asked, glancing around the room. Eric pointed to a steel rack on the wall with some clothes hangers dangling from it. On top were a couple of gray blankets and two vinyl clad pillows. He pulled them down and handed her one of each. "Ah, more vinyl," she sighed. "Glad I wore all these layers so I have something to wrap around these pillows." She busied herself with the bench until she was satisfied, but found the chair impossible to fit with a sheet. It kept slipping off. "Well, I give up!" she finally said with a hard laugh. "I think I'll just wrap myself up like a mummy when I want to sleep." She then arranged the sheet over her many layers toga-style. "Ta-da!" A rattle of the latch announced Jillian's arrival and Abby dropped the sheet and beat Eric to the door. "It's amazing how we forget how small they are when they're born!" she gushed as she took the baby out of the nurse's arms She opened the swaddling blanket. "And look – all twenty digits!"

"But no horns," Eric beamed from over her shoulder.

"Oh, you're horrible!"

"Said granny counting digits. Give me my girl."

Eric reached for his child, but the nurse had other ideas. She took Jillian out of Abby's arms and placed her in the bassinet. She pointed to the umbilical cord stump and said in broken English, "No wet. No diaper cover."

"Yes," Eric nodded and gesticulated over Jillian. "This is my second child. I know to leave the stump out to air."

The nurse nodded in return. "Good." She then marched out of the room.

Eric leaned over the bassinet. "Hey Mom, her eyes are open now."

Abby came to his side, grinning from ear to ear. "She looks like Chloe did," Abby cooed. She glanced at Eric and noticed a pained expression cross his face,

"Why wouldn't she?" he sighed.

Abby nodded and tried changing the subject. "What's in the bag from Luka?"

Eric opened the bag. "Diapers, a couple of onesies and a stuffed animal."

"You brought diapers and onesies didn't you?"

"Of course. Luka had given us a list of what to bring. But it's a nice gift."

"Yes. He and Iryna are both wonderful and they speak such good English!"

Eric nodded. "We were very lucky. Some of the posts on the surrogacy Facebook page complain about other agencies."

"Like what?"

Eric sighed. "It doesn't matter, Mom. I'll send you a link to the page and you can read them if you must know."

Abby smiled. "You're right. It doesn't matter at all. You had a wonderful experience and that's what matters. "She paused as her brain fell back into grandma mode. "What about formula?"

"Iryna is going to pump breast milk and freeze it for us."

"Oh my goodness! How wonderful of her. You mean here in the hospital?"

"Yes. But she's also going to do it at home and bring it to us every few days."

"But I thought she doesn't live here in Kyiv," Abby wondered. "Isn't that why the agency put her up in an apartment here for the last month?"

"Yeah, she lives in Bila Tserkva, about forty-five minutes away."

"She's going to drive here every few days with frozen breast milk?"

"She'll take a cab."

"You are paying her, I assume."

"For the cab. She won't take money for the breast milk or for her time."

"That's so sweet of her!"

The nurse entered again and said, "Bottle?"

"Um," Eric muttered, trying to figure out how to tell the nurse that he was waiting for Iryna's milk. He took a bottle out of the suitcase and held it up. "Breast milk?" he tried.

The nurse looked confused and walked out. She returned a couple of minutes later with another hospital employee who said, "You need to feed the baby."

"I know. We are waiting for breast milk from Iryna."

"No. Baby needs bottle now."

"Eric," Abby said in a low tone. "Did you forget that breast milk doesn't come in for a couple of days?" Abby said.

"I guess I did."

"You didn't bring any formula?"

"No . . ."

"What are we going to do?"

Eric scowled at his mother and then turned to the English-speaking woman. "Where can I get formula?"

The woman's eyes narrowed and her lips tightened into a fine line. "You have no milk?"

Eric sighed. "Is there a place I can buy some?"

"Downstairs."

When Eric didn't immediately move in that direction, she grabbed his arm. "Come!"

Abby watched them leave and then turned to her granddaughter and kissed her forehead. "Dear, dear Jillian." She took out her phone and snapped a couple more pictures. She then went over to the chair and sat down. She suddenly felt tired. Abby tried to imagine what the next two or three days would be like in this hospital room. Between Ukraine hospital protocol and Covid, she wouldn't be leaving the room at all. There was a bathroom and the little food they had bought, but no one had mentioned anything about meals brought to them. Maybe that store where Eric went to buy the formula would have something to eat. She leaned back and closed her eyes.

"Mom?" Eric said.

Abby sat up quickly. "I guess I fell asleep."

Eric smiled. "You did. I've already fed Jillian her first bottle."

"Really? I wonder how long I've been sleeping. You must be tired too."

"Not really," he answered. "I'm too wound up."

Abby smiled back and shook her head. "This is quite an experience."

Eric gazed out the window, frowning. "We are kind of in a bubble here, but Heather texted me that things are really ramping up with Russia."

"Hm. I sent Brian and Paige pictures and they didn't say anything."

"Probably don't want to alarm you, but I think we need to be vigilant about what's happening right outside our window."

Abby scowled. "I don't know why the Ukrainians are pretending everything is okay. I mean it seems so obvious. Well, what will we do?"

Eric shrugged. "I'll talk to Luka about it."

"Yes. Please do. What did Heather say?"

"She said that Russia has amassed 75% of the troops it needs to invade Ukraine and it could happen in a few weeks or tomorrow."

"Tomorrow?" Abby gulped.

"Let's not freak out until I've talked to Luka. The agency must have a plan if this happens and what they can do to help."

"I hope so. Maybe it's just a scare tactic."

"Well, that doesn't seem to be working and remember, Mom, Putin's crazy."

At that moment Jillian woke up gurgling and Abby rushed over. Jillian looked at Abby's face and Abby placed her finger in the baby's hand. Jillian squeezed it lightly and then closed her eyes and went back to sleep. Eric was standing behind her and placed his hand on her shoulder. "She is precious," Abby whispered as she patted Eric's hand.

Eric yawned. "Maybe I'll close my eyes for a bit, too."

"Should I give her more formula if she wakes up?"

"You can try."

Abby stood gazing at Jillian as Eric started snoring and then sat down on the chair/bed with her Kindle. She realized she was hungry and took out some nuts and fruit that she had quickly thrown into her purse. But just as she settled in to read and snack, she too fell back asleep.

They were startled awake when the door to the room opened and a nurse and doctor walked in. The pair went straight to the bassinet without saying a word and picked up Jillian. Abby and Eric glanced at each other, bewildered, and scrambled out of their so-called beds. The nurse and doctor spoke to each other in Ukrainian and then turned to Eric. "Diaper?" the nurse asked.

Eric took a diaper out of the bag and the nurse took it. The doctor placed Jillian on the changing table and unswaddled her. Then he took off her diaper and started checking for reflexes. Jillian started to cry and it took a lot of will power for Eric and Abby to stand and watch as these strangers examined the baby without so much as a word to them. The doctor finished the exam and left the room while the nurse turned to Eric and Abby. "You feed her?"

"Yes," Eric said. The nurse nodded and proceeded to put the clean diaper on her. He watched carefully as she swaddled Jillian. He turned to Abby. "I was never that good at this swaddling thing," he smiled.

"Me neither. Your father was much better at it." She chuckled. "More to get used to again."

The nurse started to leave. "Is, um, everything good with the baby?" Eric asked.

"Yes. Good. Healthy." She left. Eric took out his phone and texted Heather exactly what the nurse had said.

Iryna was able to squeeze out the colostrum while they waited for her regular breast milk to come in. Bland plates of unknown mush were left on the table in the hall outside the room every afternoon. Abby wouldn't touch it so Eric ate them both every day. Abby subsisted on nuts, fruit and crackers. She really wasn't hungry since she was doing nothing to work up an appetite. Jillian did what most healthy newborns did; she ate and slept.

The lack of English-speaking doctors and nurses made the daily routine somewhat awkward. They would enter the room without saying a word and do some sort of examination of Jillian and then walk out just as quietly. Eric and Abby would shrug at each other, figuring if something was wrong they would have said something. It was a godsend that Iryna spoke English and could translate, but technically they were supposed to stay separate. She brought her colostrum to their room, but didn't stay long and purposely kept her distance from Jillian.

Abby and Eric were surprised at how quickly the three days passed even though they had little to do but cuddle Jillian. They managed to sleep on the tiny "beds" though, and they had some heartfelt talks. It had been years since they'd been alone together for any length of time and they enjoyed this chance to connect. The only time they left the hospital room was to take Jillian for a hearing test, a blood test and an injection of Vitamin K. Abby watched the snow falling continually from their window, not missing being outdoors at all. They spent a lot of time texting all their friends and family and taking pictures of the mostly sleeping Jillian Irina. It ended up being a very tranquil time.

13

A COUPLE OF DAYS LATER ERIC CALLED FOR AN UBER RIDE BACK TO THE APARTMENT WHILE ABBY FUSSED OVER JILLIAN. Iryna promised to express and freeze as much breast milk as she could and bring it to them in the next couple of days. As soon as they got to the apartment, Eric called for the bassinet and stroller while Abby raided the refrigerator. They both ate pretty much everything in it while Jillian sat in her car seat on the table, studying them intently. Eric and Abby finally took their eyes off her, glanced at one another and smiled, then sighed, as they finally felt some sense of normalcy.

The Ukrainians were going about their business as if Russian troops were not poised to attack their country. The texts and emails Abby and Eric were receiving from the United States, however, told a different story. According to their friends and family, war was imminent. Eric had been texting with Luka and although he was empathetic and polite, he did not seem alarmed and offered no advice. "Let's just say," Abby suggested, "that we do have to leave as soon as possible. Will we be able to take Jillian without her having a birth certificate and passport?"

"I don't know, Mom. I've asked Luka the same question and he just says not to worry, but how can we not worry? The Covid pandemic has already made it harder to get the papers from the embassy."

"Can Heather do anything from the states?"

"She's already done her part. She had to wait for Jillian to be born so she could fill out the birth date and then fill out a form for U.S. citizens born outside the country. Then there was this other form for Jillian to get a U.S. passport."

"Did she mail them to Luka?"

"Of course, Mom," Eric replied irritably. "But first she had to jump through a few hoops because of Covid."

Abby looked perplexed. "Couldn't she just fill out the forms online?"

"She had to bring them to the Secretary of State Office and get them notarized and apostilled."

"Apostille?" Abby asked.

"It's like notarizing, but for documents outside the U.S. And the office in San Francisco that does that was closed due to Covid."

"So how did she get it done?"

"She found a place in Florida that did it for her with her electronic signature."

"Wow. She's quite resourceful!"

"Yeah she is. As soon as Luka lets me know that he got them, we can start the process here and hopefully get it rushed through."

"So—" Abby hedged, knowing she was going to irritate him further. "What exactly is the process here?"

Eric groaned. "There are fourteen documents. Do you really want me to name them all?"

"Not necessary," Abby sighed. "I just hope we can get out of here soon." At that moment Jillian started to stir. "Why don't you take a nap in the bedroom while I feed her."

Eric nodded. "Thanks, Mom."

He went into the bedroom while Abby took Jillian out of the car seat to feed her. Abby's phone was going nuts with texts and calls. She only answered Brian's and Paige's, however. "So far all is fine," she found herself texting back. She understood the Ukrainians' reluctance to face that war was imminent, but in reality she believed the news reports in the U.S. that fueled her husband's and daughter's worry and concern.

Eric and Abby tried to keep their anxiety to themselves and concentrate on Jillian. The bassinet and stroller arrived late in the afternoon. They set it up in the living room, keeping the bedroom as a sleeping sanctuary to share. They decided to wait until the next day before trying out the stroller. The doctor at the hospital had said not to take her out in temperature below twenty and when Abby looked at her weather app, it said fifteen for Kyiv. Eric decided to go out on his own. "I'll get us some dinner," he yawned. "Do you want to try some more Ukrainian food?"

Abby shrugged. "After those two days in the hospital, I think I'd rather have something like pizza. Wasn't there a pizza place a couple of blocks down, close to the underground shopping?"

"Yeah, I saw one. Okay. Any particular things you want on it?"

"You know. Just no meat or peppers, but even just a plain cheese pizza would be fine."

Eric nodded. "And a salad?"

"If they have one." Eric put on a sweatshirt and sneakers and opened the door. "Shouldn't you wear your winter coat and boots?" Abby asked. "It's fifteen degrees."

"I'm not you, Mom," Eric muttered. "I'll be fine." He left and Abby took out her computer to check the latest news. It wasn't much different from the last few days. Russia continued to put soldiers on the southern and eastern borders, and Putin still denied that he was planning to invade Ukraine. Maybe things would be fine after all. She decided to think positively. The Ukrainians would know better than the American press about what was happening in their own country, wouldn't they? Jillian was healthy and they'd get her passport and be on their way home soon.

Eric came back with pizza and salad. Jillian was still sleeping a lot so they were able to eat dinner peacefully. "Do you want to try and sleep after dinner?" Abby asked. "Or should I?"

"You can. I napped this afternoon and I'm not really tired."

"Okay. I'll try."

"Go ahead and sleep as long as you can. I'll even try and do some work."

They took turns sleeping in the bedroom and feeding Jillian. Iryna's milk finally came in well enough for her to freeze enough bags to make the taxi ride worthwhile. The weather also got warm enough to take the baby out. Well, relatively warm, but at least the temperature got over twenty. They walked and marveled more at the architecture and when it got cold, they would go into the underground shopping center. There was a park close by that bordered a river. It was filled with people who seemed totally unaware of any impending conflict.

One day two men carrying an owl and a hawk on their arms approached them on the bridge that crossed the river. They spoke Ukrainian and of course, Eric and Abby couldn't understand what they were saying. "We're Americans," Eric finally said.

Abby was on guard, worried that they were trying to rob them. Using very few English words, they pointed to the birds and one pulled out Abby's arm. The other man put the owl on her arm. That would have been weird enough, but Abby happened to be especially afraid of birds. Her arm started shaking. "No—no thank you," she cried out.

"No worry," the man pushed on. "No hurt you."

Abby looked over at Eric pleadingly, so Eric pushed his forearm toward the man. "Here, put it here," he said pointing to his own arm. The man put both birds on Eric's arm while Abby shuddered. Eric smiled and said, "Thanks. Okay. We need to go."

The man tried to keep them there, showing them some lame tricks that the birds could do. He had the hawk fly away and come back, trying to muster up some excitement from Eric and Abby, but they turned to walk away. That's when the men got even more aggressive. "You have money?" one asked.

"No, I'm sorry," Eric answered.

"You American," he responded angrily. "You have money."

"I don't have any on me," Eric responded coolly.

"Come on," the man insisted.

Abby pulled on Eric's sleeve. "Let's just go." They left and heard the men trying to accost some other unsuspecting person. "Well, that was interesting," Abby whispered as they hurried away.

"We were lucky, " Eric replied. "They were a bit insistent."

They picked up some more borscht and varenyky (the Ukrainian name for Polish pierogies or dumplings) for Abby, and holubtsi (stuffed cabbage) and piroshky (meat pie) for Eric. They sat down to eat dinner after feeding and changing Jillian. "Are you going to give Jillian a real bath tonight?" Abby asked as she cleared the table.

"I don't think so."

- - -

"Her umbilical cord fell off so she can have a real bath now."

"It's fine to keep giving her sponge baths," Eric sighed. "I'd rather wait until we get home. This kitchen sink is pretty small."

"Well, that's true," Abby mused. "I hadn't thought of that." Eric gave Jillian a sponge bath on the desk/changing table while Abby cleaned up the kitchen and called Brian. When Jillian was asleep in the bassinet, Eric went into the bedroom to call Heather. Although their respective spouses harangued them with their concerns, both Eric and Abby managed to segue the conversations to their interesting run-in with the birdmen and describing the fascinating murals that seemed to adorn every other wall.

14

THEY TOOK TURNS GETTING UP WITH THE BABY AND SLEEPING IN THE BEDROOM. A little more than a week had passed since the birth, and a routine was setting in. They waited until the warmest part of the day, around noon, to walk and shop. Eric was usually able to get some work done in the bedroom, while Abby danced and played with Jillian in the living room. She didn't get any writing done, however. When Jillian was sleeping, she slept.

Eric came out of the bedroom just as Abby finished giving Jillian her bottle. "I just got a text from Luka."

His tone caused Abby to turn to him with alarm. "What did it say? Did he get the papers?"

Eric exhaled sharply. "I don't know. It was more about what we need to do because the American embassy is closing in Kyiv."

Abby's eyes popped. "That—that must mean war is imminent."

"Apparently."

"Well," Abby sighed. "Now it can't be ignored."

"At least by us," Eric muttered.

"Luka said the embassy in Lviv will remain open for now."

"Where's that?"

"Western Ukraine, so somewhat safer than the north and the east."

"How far is Lviv?"

"I don't know exactly." He pressed some buttons on his phone. "It says the shortest driving distance is 336 miles."

"What should we do?" cried Abby. "Get an Uber and rent a hotel room?"

"I don't know, Mom!" Eric snapped.

"Well, is it closed here yet?"

"I don't know that either. Luka just wanted to give us a heads-up and will let me know when he has more information."

"If we go to Lviv, we would need to rent a bassinet and stroller there," Abby said.

"Yeah, but—oh, I need to text Iryna. She's supposed to bring breast milk tomorrow, but if we leave we can't keep it frozen."

"So we should leave now?"

"I'm not sure. We don't have to rush there if we don't need to use the embassy's services yet."

"But if there's a rush out of Kyiv, we may not get transportation." Eric said nothing. "What will you tell Iryna?"

"Just to wait until she hears from me, I guess."

"Is there enough formula?"

"I'll buy some more just to be safe."

Eric left and Abby called Brian. "Things are really heating up," Brian said. "You don't see people worried there?"

"I don't know, but the U.S. is taking no chances. They're closing the embassy!"

"Oh dear lord, Abby! You need to leave. Now."

"Oh, I know. I know." Abby took a breath, trying not to cry. "We have to get Jillian's birth certificate registered and a passport for her first, so we're thinking of moving to Lviv where the embassy is supposed to remain open."

"For God's sake!" Brian fairly yelled. "There's no time to think!" Then, more softly, "Where's that?"

"Near Poland," Abby almost whispered.

"And you would stay there instead of Kyiv?"

Abby sighed. "Hopefully, but I don't really know."

"So how long will it take?"

"I don't know!" She drew in another breath. "So how are things at home?"

"Oh, just peachy keen," Brian grumbled.

"Let Paige know that we might be moving, will you? Eric went out to get formula and food and I have to deal with Jillian. She's starting to stir." That was a lie, but she had to end this conversation immediately, before she lost control. "Love you. Bye."

— — —

Abby stared at Jillian sleeping peacefully and then took out her computer and checked out the news sites. Generally every report was bleak, if not ominous. She and Eric had to honestly discuss their options—shake Luka down for some plan of action. Thank goodness Jillian was healthy and would likely withstand a possibly perilous journey. There could be checkpoints, delays. Bombings. Yes, bombing the capital would be an easy way for Russia to bring Ukraine to its knees. Abby shuddered and hastily studied the maps again. They still seemed far away from the northern and eastern borders. She tried reassuring herself. They would have time.

"Mom?" Eric called out as he opened the front door. "Can you help me a minute?" Abby went to the door and took one of the bags. "I got you some food. See if you like it."

"We should probably eat hearty. Who knows when we'll eat again?"

"Oh Mom," Eric groaned. "There's enough drama as it is."

"Please ask Luka what we should do. I talked to Brian and he said things are escalating. If we need to go to Lviv, let's go now before we get caught in—"

"Luka will keep us posted!" Eric interrupted.

Abby bit her lip and retreated. She realized that Eric was just trying to remain calm. And dammit . . . she would too. She looked through her playlist in iTunes and found a couple of appropriate songs: Keb Mo's "Lullaby Baby Blue" and Bruce Springsteen's "Dream Baby Dream." She put them on whenever Jillian had finished a bottle and they seemed to put her to sleep quickly. Of course, it may have been that she was full and content anyway, but Abby liked to think music was magical.

They spent the next couple of days on edge, but they had heard nothing from Luka. Heather pleaded with them to contact Luka about moving to Lviv, but Eric was adamant that he wanted to wait for Luka to text him. Jillian drank formula heartily and Iryna said she had been expressing milk and should be able to come by taxi with a bunch of frozen pouches the following day. Eric told her that the U.S. embassy in Kyiv was closing and they might have to move to Lviv and she replied that Americans were overreacting.

Iryna came by taxi with frozen breast milk and said she would continue to ready the pouches for another visit. Playing with Jillian was the way they could forget about what was happening outside the apartment. Abby put on Reggae music for dancing and bouncing Jillian. They remained fairly calm until Eric received a call from Luka. "I received the paperwork from Heather, so it would be wise to prepare to go to Lviv. Do you have that document from the hospital you need for the birth certificate?"

"Yes," Eric replied.

"Meet me at the Office of Vital Records. I'll meet you there. Bring all the paperwork. I'll text you the address. I can be there at three. Bring all the paperwork."

Luka's terse manner chilled Eric. "Um . . . what arrangements should we be making for going to Lviv?"

"I'll talk to you when we meet."

"We don't need a DNA test, right?"

"Right. They've waived it because of Covid."

"Okay. Thanks, Luka."

Eric told Abby what Luka had said. "Do you need to bring Jillian with you to the office?" Abby asked.

– – –

"He didn't say to. He said he'll tell me when I see him about getting to Lviv."

"Is he still downplaying the Russian presence?"

"He didn't say anything specifically. At this point it's not about escaping a war. It's about where the U.S. Embassy is." Abby nodded although she didn't agree, and returned to scouring the Internet for news.

Eric returned from his trip to the Office of Vital Records with Jillian's birth certificate in hand. "You got it today? So fast?" Abby asked.

"Luka brought a bottle of expensive wine and that did the trick," Eric smiled.

"Smart. So what did he say about going to Lviv?"

"Not much. He's looking into it and will let me know."

Abby sighed. "I wish we knew what was happening."

"I know, Mom, but there's nothing we can do about it."

Abby opened her mouth, but Eric gave her such a cold look that she clammed up. Jillian stirred and then began to cry. Abby felt she knew the peril they were in. Eric went over and picked her up and Abby came up behind him and took her tiny hand. Both were thankful for the distraction.

15

THE NEXT AFTERNOON ABBY WAS FIDGETING IN THE VINYL CLAD EASY CHAIR AND THEN SUDDENLY BURST FORTH, "ERIC, YOU NEED TO STOP EXPECTING LUKA TO FOLLOW THROUGH. Text him!"

Eric casually looked up from his phone. "I already did,"

Abby tsked in exasperation, "When?"

"A short while ago." Eric glanced down at his phone again. "He hasn't answered yet. I was planning to tell you after I heard back from him."

Abby exhaled loudly. "I truly don't understand why the Ukrainians are hiding from the truth."

"Because they want to believe what they're told," Eric sighed. "It's human nature, especially where there's a long history of invasions and war." His phone pinged and he started to frown as he read.

"What is it?" Abby asked nervously.

"It's Luka. He says traffic is heavy from the east and trains are filling up with people going west. We should leave immediately."

"Somehow that's strangely reassuring—like I'm not crazy after all," Abby muttered. "Is he sending a car for us?"

"I'll ask him." Eric texted Luka and looked over at Jillian's bassinet. "I guess I need to text the rental company to come pick up the stroller and the bassinet."

Abby sighed. "We could use that stroller."

"We have the car seat I brought. It's more portable and versatile than the stroller anyway. Hope it isn't squeezed out of our transportation options."

"Oh!" Abby saw the worst in her mind's eye—being crushed on some train with a crying baby pressed against her and a can of formula rolling away. Formula! "Do we have enough formula?" she cried out. I mean, what if there's no store nearby where we end up staying?"

"We have enough," Eric snapped back. He got up and looked in the kitchen cupboard. "I guess. Maybe I should get some more." He returned to the living room where Abby approached him like a bird in a cage.

"Where are we going?"

"Well, *I'm* going out to buy some formula," Eric replied, "If there's any left. Even if we have to give it up along the way, maybe we can at least barter with it. You'd better start packing your things while I'm out."

What things, she wondered. Truth was there was nothing much to pack. She had been keeping her clean socks and undies in her bag, and as she handled the ones she had washed in the kitchen sink, she was thankful they were reasonably dry. She folded her extra shirt and pants and then thought of the frozen breast milk that would simply go to waste. There was some in the refrigerator, though and she heated it up, hoping she wouldn't have to wake Jillian to feed her. Fortunately she was stirring a bit by the time Abby had the milk at the proper temperature.

Abby was feeding Jillian when Eric returned with one can of formula. "Did you hear back from Luka?"

Eric nodded grimly. "He can't find us a car. He recommends using Uber."

"It'll cost a fortune."

"Do you want to try and navigate a crowded train system with a two week old baby in a foreign country where we don't speak the language?"

Abby sighed. "Well, I'm packed. Did you reach the rental company?"

"They haven't answered. We can't wait around for them, anyway."

"Did you tell the woman who owns this apartment? Maybe she can be here when they come to pick up the stuff."

"I haven't texted her yet." He took out his phone and started toward the bedroom.

"Have you told Heather what's going on?" Abby called to him.

"No." He stopped and turned to look at his mother. "Have you told Brian?"

"No." They nodded at each other in tacit agreement that telling them would only serve to worry them both. "What about Uber?" Abby quickly added.

"I requested the ride but they haven't given me an ETA."

"What did you give them as the destination in Lviv? Did Luka give you any ideas of hotels?"

"I just gave them the address of the embassy. I'm hoping they will be able to help us find a hotel."

Abby started dressing Jillian warmly as Eric packed his backpack and then they both started rounding up the baby equipment. Abby then went into the kitchen and came back to the living room with a shopping bag full of snacks and water bottles. "You know we can't carry all this stuff," Eric said. "

Abby sagged and dropped the shopping bag on the floor. "What?"

"I'm saying that we don't know what's in store for us in Lviv—let alone what's in store for us just getting there. People are getting desperate. We might not have the Uber to ourselves. Maybe we need a backup plan."

 "Can't you call Uber?"

"I don't know. But chances are they wouldn't speak English anyway. The app is the only way I've ever done it. I'll try Luka again and see if he can point us in a direction."

"I know Luka has his own family to consider, but you have paid the agency a lot of money. They need to help us too."

"Yes, Mom," Eric retorted. He texted Luka and then turned to Abby. "Look, sorry—"

"Don't," Abby replied, reaching out for his arm. "We can't waste our energy on hurt feelings and apologies."

Eric managed a little smile. "Mom—" His phone pinged.

"Is it Luka?"

Eric looked at his phone. "Yes. He's tracking a lead on another car service. He'll give them the address of a hotel he's heard of in Lviv. He said he'll work at getting us a car service and have them take us to a hotel he knows of in Lviv."

"Do you think he'll be able to get us a car?"

Eric shrugged. "Hope so. At least we have two maybes now."

"Did you call the company about picking up the baby stuff again? And the landlady?"

"I will now." He went into the bedroom as Jillian started to cry.

Abby picked her up and comforted her. "Oh sweet baby. What a beginning to your life you are having."

Eric returned a few minutes later. "I reached the landlady and told her what was happening. She was very nice about it all. She said to leave the stuff and give the rental company her number and she will let them in."

"How are we going to heat up the formula for Jillian?" Abby asked. "It's ten degrees outside."

"I guess we can put the can on the floor next to a heater vent."

Abby gave him a dubious look. "We should probably wait to feed her until we are almost ready to leave and maybe the car ride will keep her asleep. How far is it again?"

"I think a six or seven hour drive in the best of times."

"Oh Jeez!" Abby scoffed. "So are we ready to go as soon as we hear from Luka?"

"I have my stuff and Jillian's ready. Are you?"

"Yep. So now we just wait for Luka." Eric took Jillian out of Abby's arms and cooed at her. Abby took out her computer and went to a news source to try and find out if anything new had happened. "Russia is focusing mostly on the eastern border, but fortifying the north too."

"Does it say anything about Kyiv specifically?"

"Just that it's the capital and it's where the president is so of course it's also a target."

"I guess they could just use airplanes to bomb it." Eric exhaled loudly and shook his head. "We're not far from many of the civic buildings. I wonder if the president's office is nearby too."

They fell silent for a while. Eric kept glancing at his phone to see if Luka had texted. Finally Abby said, "Should you try that Uber app again?"

"Yeah." Eric did that and then said, "Maybe we should also be looking at the possibility of taking a bus or a train."

"How would we get to the train station if we can't get Uber to respond?"

"It would be a short ride to the train station. It might be that they can't find any drivers willing to go all the way to Lviv and that's why they haven't answered before."

"I'm starting to get pretty damn anxious about this," Abby fretted.

Eric didn't answer, but he did take out his phone and tried the Uber app again. As he was typing, his phone dinged with a message from Luka. "Good news. He found someone willing to drive us to Lviv. The car will be here in about half an hour."

"Oh hooray!" Abby exclaimed.

"Luka did say it will cost us much more than Uber would."

"At this point that hardly matters! Did he say the name of the hotel?"

"No." Eric texted again and waited for a response, but none came.

"I wish Luka would answer your texts more promptly."

"He's not just dealing with us, Mom. He has other people I'm sure that are either here to pick up babies or coming soon. Not to mention he has to deal with the surrogates and find places for them to stay."

"Should we tell Heather and Brian yet?"

"Yeah, probably."

"At least we have some information to give them, so that might relieve some of their worry," Abby replied. They both texted and then looked at the pile of bags and the car seat. "Do you think we have too much stuff to be schlepping around?"

"What should we do? Leave some clothes or something?" Eric asked.

"I don't know," Abby answered. "Let's just wait and see if the driver balks at taking all of it.

Maybe he's escaping to Lviv too and has his own stuff."

They texted Heather and Brian and then both their phones rang simultaneously. They smiled at each other, figuring that's what would happen. Abby went into the bedroom to talk to Brian and Eric stayed in the living room to talk to Heather. Eric was feeding Jillian a bottle when Abby emerged from the bedroom. "She just finished," Eric said handing the bottle to Abby and putting Jillian on his shoulder to burp her.

Abby took the bottle to the kitchen to wash it. "Where should I put this?" she asked as she came out with the bottle. Eric pointed to one of the bags. He changed Jillian's diaper, dressed her as warmly as he could, and strapped her into her car seat.

"Well, I guess we should go downstairs and wait. You take Jillian and your purse. I'll carry the rest of the bags."

Abby nodded and got her coat, hat and gloves on. She put her purse over her shoulder and picked up the car seat. She and Eric looked into each other's eyes and they both sighed. "Good luck to us," murmured Abby.

16

THE DRIVER SKILLFULLY THREADED THE CAR THIS WAY AND THAT ON THE BACK STREETS OF KYIV, TRYING TO AVOID THE WORST OF THE TRAFFIC. "Wish we could say this was just rush hour," muttered Abby as she watched people go to and fro on the sidewalks. It seemed everyone had some place to go, and there were signs of evacuating, with people pulling wagons or pushing strollers full of belongings.

"Very busy," the driver replied. "People leaving."

"I guess the propaganda isn't working anymore," mused Abby. "Even our secretary of state says to leave the country, not just Kyiv."

 "Well we can't leave until we get Jillian's passport," Eric replied irritably.

"At this point that's the embassy's job," grumbled Abby. "I just hope all these people on the road aren't looking for a room in Lviv."

"Most of them probably have better options, like friends or family in the country."

Abby poked the driver. "What hotel are you taking us to?" The driver just kept his eyes on the street ahead and shrugged. Either he didn't want to be bothered or he didn't understand. "Well, you better not dump us on some street corner with a two week old baby!" The frown that passed over the driver's face was not reassuring. "Eric, text Luka and find out what hotel we're going to."

Eric sighed and pulled out his phone to text Luka. Meanwhile, Jillian started to cry. "She can't be hungry yet," he said.

Abby turned to Jillian and fussed with her. "She's a baby. She's just crying."

"She's probably picking up on all our apprehension," Eric said. Abby soothed her and the car was quiet for a while. Eric kept glancing at his phone to see if Luka had texted back.

"Maybe we should find a hotel ourselves?" Abby asked. "Like hotels dot com or something?"

"I'll try." Eric hit some keys on his phone. "No internet," he sighed.

"Should we go with the original plan of going to the embassy?" Abby asked.

"It will be the middle of the night when we get there," Eric replied. "I doubt they'll be open."

Abby looked out the window. "With this traffic it'll be morning before we get there. How long have we been on the road?"

"Two hours," Eric answered. "And I think we've gone all of ten miles."

Another hour went by and the traffic only got slower. "We need to change her diaper and try to warm a bottle," Eric finally said.

"I could use a bathroom too," Abby added. "Can we stop at the next restaurant or gas station?" Abby asked the driver.

The driver got off the highway in the town of Nebelytsia and found a petrol station. They all got out of the car and hustled inside. There was a long line to use the restroom. "You wait in line, Mom. I'll see if I can get them to heat up this bottle."

The line moved fairly quickly. People were trying to be considerate, but in the rush the restroom was dirty and all the supplies were gone. For once Abby was happy she was wearing a mask. She fished through her purse for some Kleenex and was out of there as soon as possible. Eric was standing there waiting for her, gingerly holding a big paper cup.

"It was the best they could do," explained Eric. "Hot water from the espresso machine. That's all they have left. Hot water. I was lucky to get the cup—the baby bottle was key to getting anything at all."

"Is it a clean cup?"

"Mom . . ." he started to turn back toward the car.

"Don't you need to use the restroom?"

"I followed our driver out back. That's where all the men are going."

"Oh God," groaned Abby. She started fumbling with her purse. "Let me get you some sanitizer." He kept moving so she had to trot to catch up to him.

"Mom, I've got to get this to the car before my fingers fry."

"You can't mix formula in water that hot!"

"It'll cool as I change her diaper," Eric retorted. He opened the door and laid Jillian on the set to change her diaper. As he slipped the soiled diaper out from underneath her the driver started the motor. "Not yet," Eric snapped. He could see the driver glance into the rear view mirror, his nose curled. The motor went silent. Eric handed the dirty diaper to Abby, who gingerly wandered off looking for somewhere to dispose of it. Eric cleaned Jillian up and put on a clean diaper.

Abby returned. "The trash is overflowing."

"So are the roads, Mom. Just do your best."

"I did," she sighed, taking out her sanitizer. "I guess. Here," she said, holding the little bottle downward for a squeeze.

After cleaning his hands Eric eyeballed what looked like the correct amount of water, measure out some powder into the big paper cup and stirred it with a straw. "Here, pour this into her bottle as I strap Jillian into her seat," he directed. Once Jillian was secure Eric started to say something to the driver, but he was already on it and started the motor again. Eric and Abby got in on either side of Jillian, and Abby started feeding her.

"Have you heard from Luka?" Abby murmured.

Eric looked at his phone. "Nope. I'll try again in a little while."

Abby nervously looked over the driver's shoulder at the gas gauge. It seemed that little if any gas had been put into the car during their stop. Up ahead the road was now fairly clear, but narrow and dodging around farms and through villages. Under different circumstances she would have thought it pretty. She looked over at Eric and his eyes were closed, as if shutting out the present. She decided to do the same, although she had no intention of dozing off. But sleep she did. She was jarred awake by the car coming to an abrupt stop. "Wh-what's happening?"

"We came upon a curve and suddenly came up on all these cars," Eric replied. He looked at his phone. "We're near a place called Rivne."

Abby yawned. "How long have we been on the road?"

"About eight hours. So much for getting to Lviv in about six."

"How much further?"

Eric studied his phone again and frowned. "Three hours under normal circumstances."

Abby took out her phone and read several texts, shaking her head. "Both Brian and Paige say Russia has upped the ante considerably," she sighed. "Americans are supposed to leave Ukraine."

Eric scowled. "I told you, we can't leave without a passport for Jillian."

"Don't you think under the circumstances they would waive that?"

"I don't know, Mom. Maybe if there is in fact a war starting—"

"But a war is starting!" Abby snapped. "Brian said weapons have been fired numerous times in the eastern part of the country."

"Yeah, I saw that. But we are going to the most western city in Ukraine. The Russians are mobilizing in the north, south and east."

Abby exhaled loudly. "At this rate who knows when we're going to get to Lviv." The car started inching ahead.

"Well, at least we're warm and finally moving again," Eric murmured. Soon the car passed a minor accident with two men yelling at one another on the side of the road. Jillian stirred and grimaced at the disturbing sound. Eric took her out of the car seat and held her. "Probably time for her to eat and get a diaper change, anyway." He tapped the driver on the shoulder. "Could you stop at the next gas, I mean, petrol station?"

The driver didn't answer, but Eric detected a slight nod. It took awhile to find an open station, and although busy and only premium petrol was available, the situation seemed less dire. Abby stuffed some take out paper napkins in her coat pocket and went to the restroom while Eric took the bottle over to a snack bar. By the time Abby returned Eric had Jillian changed and was stirring formula in a large cup. "I had to buy a latte to get a cup of hot water, but at least I got a spoon." Abby shook her head, but also managed a chuckle. "I also got us some granola bars and a bottle of water," Eric continued. "Well, at least I think they're snack bars. I don't think they'd sell dog biscuits here. Anyway, you're just going to have to be less picky right now."

Abby laughed. "I already decided that."

They got back on the road after Eric fed Jillian and they settled in for what they hoped would be just a three-hour drive. Traffic was now light, being past midnight, but that only made it harder to follow the correct route, so their speed didn't increase much overall. They slowed for most every crossroad as the driver scanned the signs. "Are you okay to keep driving?" Eric asked the driver. Again, just a slight nod as an answer. Eric and Abby both raised their eyebrows and shrugged. Then they both closed their eyes again, hoping the drone of the engine and the swaying of the car would lull them asleep.

They must have been dozing at least some of the time because as the car came to another stop Abby opened her eyes and saw dawn glimmering in the east and a line of cars ahead. "Well, I guess I can rule out rush hour in the Bay area as the worst," Abby moaned. She looked over at Eric who was staring ahead. "Do you know where we're at?"

"Sorta. I haven't had a signal for a while. The last I knew we were forty kilometers from Lviv."

"Your phone isn't working?"

"It's working, Mom. Coverage is just spotty."

"Well, how far is forty kilometers?"

"Mm, maybe twenty-five miles. I think we've traveled about a third of that."

"Thank goodness. We're almost there. Did you ever hear from Luka about the hotel?"

"No, I didn't," Eric sighed. "Now that it's morning I think we should just go to the embassy and let them help us."

Abby nodded. "That's probably a better idea."

It took an hour and a half to get to what was now the American embassy in Lviv. They wearily got out of the car and Eric tipped the driver handsomely. A big grin passed over the driver's face and he heartily shook Eric's hand before jumping back into the car. They trudged into the building with all their belongings and found no one sitting at the reception desk. "Hmm," Eric said. "I wonder where everyone is. It looks pretty deserted in here."

A woman came out of an office. "Can I help you?" Eric started to explain who they were and why they were there, but she cut him short.

"There are only a handful of us here right now. All American citizens have been told to leave Ukraine."

Eric and Abby glanced at one another in dismay, and then Eric said, "Um, we have a two-week old baby and she needs a passport."

"We just took a very long ride to get here because they closed the embassy in Kyiv!" Abby interjected. "What are we supposed to do?"

The woman sighed, studied Jillian for a moment and then shrugged. "I don't know how to help expedite getting your baby a passport."

"Well, if you don't know, can you try and find someone who does?" Abby implored.

"Give me your phone number and I'll call you when I have some information."

Eric gave her his phone number and then asked, "Is there a place for us to stay nearby?"

"And you will call or text very soon with information?" Abby cut in.

She nodded. "I'll do my best, but communications are poor right now and we have no idea if we might be pulled out in a few hours or a few days. Most of our superiors have left the building to help get their families out of the country. There's a hotel just down the street. You'll see it."

Abby shivered and dared not look at Eric. "Come on, Mom," he said dejectedly. They picked up all their stuff and walked out. When they arrived at the hotel they initially had a hard time getting anything out of the clerk behind the desk, but eventually a manager got involved and her kindness seemed genuine.

"Well, here we are," Abby said as she plopped her suitcase on a bed and went over to the radiator to warm her hands. "If this was a pleasure trip I'd be impressed by this room for that price."

"I'm just happy we got a room at all," Eric muttered as he looked through his wallet. "Credit cards might not work much longer."

Abby glanced over at Eric to see how serious he was, but a wail from Jillian saved her the trouble of asking and she was thankful for the diversion. She went over and took her out of the car seat. "What a trooper she's been!"

Eric came up and took her from his mother's arms. "She's been incredible," he grinned, making a goofy face at her.

"You were a very easy baby too," Abby smiled.

Jillian and Abby lay down while Eric went out searching for a grocery store or a restaurant. They were fast asleep when Eric returned with two pizzas: one with meat for him and a vegetarian for Abby. It was the closest place to the hotel and he knew that they were both hungry enough to eat cold pizza if need be. Eric ate his and pondered their predicament, realizing that if they had to actually evacuate Ukraine, they'd likely be eating anything they could find. His mother would have little if any choice in the matter.

Eric lay down on the other bed after finishing his pizza and closed his eyes. They both slept for another hour or so when they were awakened by Jillian wailing. They both rushed over to her car seat and Abby watched as Eric tried to soothe her. "Do we have any more formula?" Abby asked.

"Yeah, in the suitcase."

Abby went over and took out a clean bottle and a box of dried formula. "How are we going to warm this?"

"Is there a coffee machine? Maybe just put water in it and then heat the bottle with the water?"

"Put the bottle in what container?"

"I don't know!" Eric snapped. "The ice bucket?"

Abby looked around. "I don't see an ice bucket. Ice may not be a thing in this part of the world."

"How about if I put hot water from the coffee maker in the bottle with some powder and give it a shake?"

"Said the man," sighed Abby. "If you shake hot water it explodes all over the place. And it'll probably taste like coffee and not be sanitary, but I don't see that we have a choice. Even putting bottled water in the machine is a risk, but I don't trust the tap water more. Remember Chernobyl?"

"No."

"The nuclear power plant in Ukraine that leaked? I think it was in the mid or late eighties."

"How would I remember that? I was like five at the time!"

"Well, the tap water could be radioactive."

"Okay, Mom, now you're just being paranoid," growled Eric. "No one is glowing in the dark here. You don't even know where Chernobyl is, let alone where the water supply for Lviv comes from!"

"I think Chernobyl is north of Kyiv . . ." Abby mused, then spouted, "I hope the Russians don't do something to the nuclear power plants!"

"Stop, Mom. Just stop. We have enough to deal with without worst-case scenarios. Go down to the front desk and see if you can get some bottled water—and try to clear your mind in the process!"

A hurt expression passed over Abby's face and then she forced a smile. "Good idea," she said, patting his shoulder and left.

Eric went over to the coffee maker and sniffed. It seemed clean enough, but it did smell like coffee. That was just the basket, though. He poured some water into the machine and ran it without the basket and its aim was somewhat reliable into a paper cup. "It is what it is," he muttered to himself. "I could mix just a little formula in the cup so I don't waste it. No way to store leftovers anyway and it'll be easier to clean the bottles."

Abby returned with two bottles of water. "They said water isn't safe to drink in Ukraine for lots of reasons, not just Chernobyl," she reported a little too brightly. "I guess that's why we had that water dispenser in the apartment."

"Well, that's honest of them," Eric replied with a touch of sarcasm. He poured out the hot water from the coffee maker into the sink and turned to her. "Did you just buy two bottles of water then? We'll need way more than that."

"They gave me two bottles," corrected Abby. We can buy more at a grocery store."

Eric took a bottle and poured some of the cold water into the coffee maker and then a little in a cup, mixing it with the powder and then passing the cup under the sputtering coffee maker. A finger test. "Ouch!" He winced as the coffee maker scalded him and put more cold water in.

"Remember when you won first place at the Science Fair?" Abby chirped.

"Somehow that doesn't improve my confidence." He dipped a finger in again and it seemed about right.

"Is that all you're making?"

"Yes, Mom. We have no way to store leftovers. I can make more if she's still hungry."

"Practical," Abby replied cautiously, "but that might make her fussy."

And she won't be the only one," Eric said, handing the bottle over to her.

Abby pursed her lips, took the bottle and went over to feed Jillian. She had a small triumph when it was clear that wasn't enough to satisfy Jillian. At first she thought distraction would work as Eric mixed more formula, but Jillian's protests grew louder, so Abby carried her over to watch while she made up a song about daddy making her a bottle. Jillian made faces and snorted, but seemed to have some understanding of the situation. "Such a smart baby," Abby cooed.

"I'll feed her this time," Eric said, reaching for Jillian. "Go eat your pizza."

Abby smiled and went over to open the box. "What kind did you get me?"

"No meat . . . no peppers. By inspection, that's all I know."

"Hmm," she said as she took a bite. "I guess it's just cheese and tomato, but that's perfect."

She ate while Eric fed Jillian. When they finished, Abby took out her phone and opened iTunes. "I'm going to put on some Bob Marley," she announced. "I've noticed Jillian likes Reggae." She took Jillian and danced around the room with the smiling baby while Eric washed the bottle. They spent the next hour or so playing with Jillian and texting their families, but downplaying the unknowns of their situation. Finally, Jillian fell asleep and their gaze settled on one another, both on the verge of starting the inevitable discussion. Eric opened his mouth, but Abby cut him off. "Oh, let's not. It's been such a nice few hours." Eric registered surprise and she managed to chuckle. "Surprise, surprise. Your mother is in a look for the silver lining moment."

"Glad to hear it, Mom," he smiled.

Abby went over to him and kissed his forehead. "I'm going to lay down for a while. Goodnight, son."

"Goodnight, Mom."

Jillian woke up a couple of times through the night and they took turns feeding her. After they'd showered and dressed, Eric texted Luka about the latest snags in getting a passport, hoping he might have some connections or insight. Since it was a balmy minus three Celsius, Abby agreed she'd survive and that it was a good time to give Jillian some fresh air.

They found a grocery store and bought a few items that didn't require refrigeration and were light to carry, in case they had to leave at a moment's notice. "I feel like we're on a backpacking trip," Abby said as they paid for the granola bars, nuts, and fruit. Eric threw in some beef jerky as well, but the bottled water is what took up the most room. Most importantly, they bought some premixed formula bottles to use during travel.

They strolled around the downtown streets, trying to lose themselves in the act of sightseeing. The architecture was similar to Kyiv's, and they stopped to study the details. Statues, both traditional and whimsical, seemed to be around every corner. They walked past a few museums and a large number of cafes, but Covid and a two-week old baby kept them from entering any of them. Abby tried to keep her whining about the cold to a minimum, much to Eric's surprise. He finally asked her, "Are you doing okay walking around?"

"Well, my hands are ready to fall off, even though I'm wearing two pairs of gloves!"

"You're a real trooper," Eric smiled.

"Gee, you sound like you mean that."

"I do mean that."

"Somehow I don't believe you. But anyway, if Jillian can do it, I can do it."

"She doesn't know any better," Eric laughed.

Abby laughed with him. "It sure feels good to banter with you, like nothing is unknown or frightening."

Eric sighed. "We do need to make some definite plans. I'm sure you've been thinking about it, too."

"Yes," Abby replied tentatively. And what have you come up with?"

"Well, I'll keep trying to contact Luka and we should go to the consulate again tomorrow and look pitiful. I think our persistent presence would be the best motivator"

"You mean like camp out in the lobby?"

"Just for the day," he grinned. "We have our snacks and premixed formula."

"And we'll have a dirty diaper or two," Abby grinned mischievously. "That should be a good motivator."

17

February 24, 2022

RELENTLESS PINGING FROM BOTH THEIR PHONES ROUSED THEM FROM A DEEP SLEEP. "What time is it?" moaned Abby.

Bleary eyed, Eric swiped the screen on his phone. "Six," he muttered. Jillian let out a wail as he opened the text. He let out a grunt of surprise. "We're in for it."

Abby rolled out of bed and went for Jillian. "What? Wait—"

"Yes," Eric replied.

Abby veered away from Jillian and went straight to her laptop. Eric frowned, pushed himself out of bed and went over to Jillian. "They're invading from the north, south and east boundaries," Abby cried. "They've bombed the airport in Kyiv."

Eric picked up Jillian and gently rocked her. "We should be alright here in the west for a while, but they will want to cut off escape routes."

"Don't say that!" Abby cried. She kept looking through her computer for more information. "When does the consulate open?"

"I don't know. Probably nine."

"Please try Luka again!"

"I will after I go down to the front desk," Eric replied, handing Jillian over to Abby and grabbing his clothes.

"Right," Abby affirmed. "We need to know what to do. I mean if they do start bombing here. Oh my God! I can't believe we're in a war zone!"

"Yes, yes," Eric hissed, stumbling into his pants. "Turn on the coffee maker so I can make Jillian's bottle."

Abby turned on the coffee maker. "I can do it. Go down to the front desk now."

"Are you sure?" Eric asked, pushing his hair back with his hands.

"I've been watching you do it. Go!"

"Okay, okay," he said, dashing to the door.

Abby was feeding Jillian when Eric returned, breathless. "The lobby is full of people and there's like at least three languages going at once," he gasped. "The nearest bomb shelter isn't far, but I'm not sure I understood exactly where it is."

"Are we supposed to go there now?" Abby asked frantically.

"No, only if the sirens go off."

"This is crazy!"

"Mom, please. Try to stay calm. I'll walk over to the consulate and see if they have any advice."

Eric left and Abby called Brian back. "Oh thank God you're alright!" he bellowed into the phone.

"Nothing is happening here in Lviv, yet. I think we're okay for now."

"You need to come home."

"We can't just leave, Brian," she explained with some annoyance. "We need a passport for Jillian first. And we have to figure out how. I'm sure the consulate can help us." Abby found it strange that she was reassuring Brian when she was petrified herself.

"I'm sure not every person crossing the borders into Poland and Hungary and Romania have passports!" Brian snapped back.

"Well we still have to get to the border and cross it with a two-week old baby in freezing temperatures. That's not exactly an easy task!"

"I know, I know." Brian's voice dropped. "I'm just so damn worried."

"So are we," Abby replied, her voice cracking. "I'll let you know as soon as we have some answers." She hung up and pressed her phone to her chest. She took a deep breath and glanced down at her phone, swiping over the screen. She opened iTunes, put on Bob Marley and then she and Jillian danced around the room.

Eric got to the building where the consulate office was to find it locked and empty. A sign on the door said they were closed until further notice. "No!" he cried, banging on the glass with his fists. He looked around for a phone number to call in emergencies, but found nothing. He took out his phone to text Luka, but decided things were getting to the point that a phone call would be more in order. But, of course, it just went to voicemail. "Luka, we need to know what to do!" he shouted frantically into the phone. "The consulate here in Lviv is closed. Please call me back right away!"

He dreaded going back to the hotel with the bad news. He stood at their door, listening to Bob Marley seeping through. Opening it, Abby swung around, pulling Jillian close to her. "What did they say?"

"They're closed," he murmured.

"Is it too early? Maybe they open at ten."

Eric shook his head. "There's a sign that says they're closed until further notice."

Abby took in a deep breath and exhaled slowly. "Well . . . I guess we are on our own."

"I'd better call Heather," Eric sighed.

"I spoke to Brian. He's worried sick and wants us to leave right now."

"I'm sure Heather will say the same thing."

"I think they're right," Abby murmured. "So . . . what now?"

Eric shrugged. "I haven't heard from Luka. He's probably in a bomb shelter, anyway."

Abby sighed. "First of all, we have to go out and find people who know where to go *and* speak English."

"We have the translator on our phone," Eric reminded her.

"Is it too cold for Jillian?"

"We can wrap her up in blankets."

"Call Heather while I get dressed," Abby directed as she took out a comb from her purse and ran it through her hair. "She's probably freaking out by now." That she was, although Eric voice was some assurance to her that all was okay for the moment.

They wrapped Jillian up in blankets and they set out to explore the neighborhood. They were pleasantly surprised to find that people were going about their business as if there was no war going on. They stopped and bought some coffee and sweet rolls. Eric asked the barista if she spoke English. She shook her head, but pointed to a customer. Eric walked over to the customer. "Do you speak English?"

"A little," he answered.

"We are Americans. We want to know how to get across the border into Poland."

"Look for all the people," he laughed. Eric was taken aback at his nonchalant attitude. "Russia in south and east. Not here. People running are from those places."

"You're not worried that they will attack here?"

The man shook his head. "If they do, I go to bomb shelter." The man took out his phone and showed Eric a map of six thousand bomb shelters in Lviv. "Close one is in basement here." The man pointed to a building near their hotel.

"Thank you very much." Eric told Abby what the man had shown him.

"Is that the same one the hotel clerk said?" Abby asked.

"I think so."

"Maybe we need to talk to them again."

"Yes. I think you're right." They started walking back to the hotel. "Let's stop and get some more groceries," he added as they passed a small store.

They arrived back at the hotel and brought their supplies back to the room. "I'll feed Jillian while you go down and talk to the front desk clerk again."

He left while Abby took Jillian out of her car seat and changed her as she warmed a bottle. She looked at the bags and sighed. There was no way they could bring all this if they were going to be without a car and driver. She fed Jillian and tried to be upbeat, putting on some more reggae music. The baby smiled and Abby decided that reggae was definitely a favorite.

When Eric arrived a few minutes later, he found Abby and Jillian dancing around the room again. "The clerk said that the train station is crowded with people trying to get across the border. But like the man in the café said, they are mostly people from places in the south and east.”

“But Americans are being told to leave.”

“Yes, she did mention that.”

They looked at each other and nodded. “I guess we need to heed their advice,” Abby replied. “Even without a passport for Jillian.”

“I still want to talk to Luka. Let’s give it another night here at the hotel.”

“It’s hard to argue with a warm bed and bathroom.”

“I just hope I don’t regret it in the morning,” sighed Eric. Abby frowned, so Eric added, “We can try to get a handle on the situation, at least. Do some research on our phones and laptops.”

They pored over their devices, trying to track ways to the border. After a while, they simply started by looking at the date line. If the source was more than a day or two old, they didn’t bother reading it. The one obvious thing in their research was that things were changing at a moment’s notice.

That evening Eric finally got a text from Luka, but it was vague—only saying that he was trying his best to get leads for them to get out of the country. Eric relayed the message to his mother, trying to sound upbeat. Abby just nodded as she studied his anxious eyes. It would be a long, restless night.

18

THE SCREECH OF SIRENS BROKE OUT JUST BEFORE DAWN. Abby woke up screaming, "Oh my God!"

Jillian joined in the wailing and Eric instinctively jumped out of bed to go to her. He grabbed her and went to the window to see people rushing outside and down the street. "I guess we need to get to that shelter!"

"Do we just go and leave our stuff here?" Abby cried.

Eric shrugged. "There's no time. Just grab formula and bottles of water as I get her ready!" They rushed around the room, occasionally getting in each other's way as Abby threw her computer and phone into her bag along with formula, water, bottles and diapers. They ran out the door and soon joined the other guests scrambling out of the hotel lobby. They didn't need to figure out how to get to the shelter. They just followed the throngs who were being herded with shouts and gesticulations by someone who seemed to know what to do. Eric caught up to the man, "Do you speak English?"

"Come with us," he answered.

"Are they bombing Lviv?" Eric asked.

"Near. Not right here." Abby and Jillian caught up just as he again rushed forward.

"What did he say?" she asked.

"Some bombs have gone off near town."

They got to the building where the shelter was and followed the crowd down to the basement. There was nothing to do but sit on the floor along with the others and wait. They fed Jillian and nodded at the people who looked at them with pity. There were children, but none as young as Jillian. Everyone looked frightened and morose at the same time and many were weeping. There was little conversation. Luckily, there was a restroom, but with so many people there, the lines were always long. Cell service and Internet were spotty, but they worked some.

After a few hours, people started getting restless and there was murmuring among them. Abby and Eric tried to decipher what people were saying by holding up his phone, hoping the translator app would pick up the words and put them into English. A child about twelve came over to Eric and asked in Ukrainian what he was doing. "I'm American . . ." Eric began, faltering as he tried to explain himself.

"Oh speak English?" the boy responded.

"Yes. Do you?"

"I learn in school. Not good."

"Can you tell me what everyone is talking about? I am trying to translate with my phone all the talk about sirens."

The boy looked at him quizzically. "The sirens mean bombs."

"I know. I wondered if there was any more news about the bombs. Are they hitting Lviv?"

"Near here."

"Are you from Lviv?"

The boy shook his head. "Odesa. I come with mother and sister. Father stay there to fight. Why you here?"

Eric pointed to Abby and Jillian. "My baby was born in Kyiv. We are trying to take her home to America."

"Why you have baby in Kyiv?"

Eric smiled. What should he say? Certainly he couldn't go into the whole story with a young boy. "Uh, my wife couldn't have a baby herself."

"Oh. So you adopt baby here."

"Not exactly."

The boy looked at Abby and then said," Your wife too old to have baby."

Eric laughed hard at that one. "That's my mother."

The boy smiled. "Not wife?"

"My wife couldn't come because she had Covid."

The boy nodded. Finally he seemed to understand something. Eric noticed that some people were packing up their things and walking toward the stairs and a woman was waving at the boy. "I think we go now."

"Are you staying in Lviv?"

The boy shrugged. "I don't know. We wait here for now."

"Could you ask your mother if it's safe to leave now?"

The boy ran up to his mother and then ran back. "She say war not here, but coming."

"Thank you. I guess we'll leave too." The boy ran back to his mother. Eric turned to Abby. "Did you hear all that?"

"He's adorable. I liked the way you handled explaining Jillian and me," she winked.

"I didn't know what to say."

"Well, you did well. And I'm flattered that he thought I was your wife, even though I looked too old to have a baby. Should we go back to the hotel and plan?"

Eric nodded and put Jillian back into her car seat. They followed the group walking toward the stairs and soon, most of the rest of them got up and joined in. When they got outside and walked to the hotel, they noticed a multitude of people and cars lined up at stores and ATM machines. The sirens had stopped wailing and if it weren't for the anxious faces of people rushing around and in the cars jamming the streets, one would have thought it was a normal day in Lviv.

They arrived at the hotel and Eric immediately called Luka, but as usual, it went to voicemail. "This is getting scarier and scarier!" Abby moaned. "We could get stranded and our phones won't work. Then what would we do?"

"Let's try not to freak out too much," Eric replied, trying not to sound terrified.

"How can we not freak out? We could be killed, for God's sake!"

Eric had a hard time coming up with something to ease their panic. "I think we should shower and eat and be prepared to leave," he said as he took Jillian out of the car seat. "We don't know what's going to happen, but we can't stay here.

"I wish Luka would give us some direction," Abby grumbled.

"We can't rely on him right now. He's got his hands full."

"Aren't we his responsibility too?"

"Whether we are or not doesn't matter anymore. We are intelligent adults and we just have to come up with a plan."

Abby exhaled sharply and nodded. "Okay. What's your idea?"

"Let's just figure out where the train station is and go there."

"And then go where?"

"People are crossing the border into Poland, Romania, Hungary . . ."

"Which is closest?" Abby asked.

"Poland." Eric looked around the room. "But we can't take all this on the train. We'll need to leave a lot of our clothes and stuff. Most important is Jillian's formula and bottles." He smiled at Abby. "And your computer. Go ahead and shower first. I'll get the paperwork together that we'll need when we get to Poland."

Abby went into the bathroom and Eric packed his backpack with the papers and the formula and bottles. He put in an extra blanket for Jillian and some diapers. He put the remaining diapers on top of Abby's large purse so she could bring them. It was obvious that he and Abby would be wearing the same clothes for quite a while. "Okay, my turn," Eric said as he handed Jillian to his mother. "Just pack those diapers and maybe whatever food and water we have in one bag."

"Okay. I'll change and feed her. So we're not going to take both suitcases?"

"I don't know. We can try to pack one of them with clothes and stuff, but we might need to leave it somewhere. Put everything important in your purse."

In fifteen minutes they were ready to go. "Do we just leave the suitcase with extra stuff here in the room?" Abby asked.

"Let's bring it down to the front desk and see if they have a idea. I hate to just throw out perfectly good clothes and things when there are people here who could probably use them."

"There were several homeless people in that bomb shelter. Maybe we should leave the suitcase there for them. They're probably the only ones that are going to stay in that shelter."

"Good idea, Mom." Eric glanced at his phone, hoping for some word from Luka. "I guess we just find the train station ourselves." He looked at the map app, trying to decipher where they were and where the train station was, but it was too confusing in Ukrainian. "The front desk clerk should be able to point us in the right direction," he finally said.

"Are we going to walk there?"

"I can try Uber. But first let's see how far it is." They went to the front desk and the clerk told them that it would be difficult getting there with the baby. Eric used the Uber app, but it didn't respond. "Do you have any other suggestions?" Eric asked the clerk. The clerk shrugged. "Maybe someone driving give you ride."

Eric went back to find Abby sitting with the two suitcases and car seat. "Okay. Let's start walking," he said. "We're not going to get there any other way."

"Is the bomb shelter on the way?"

"Yeah, close enough." They walked back to the building and Eric went down into the shelter with the one suitcase. He saw a couple, huddled in a corner with sleeping bags. He wasn't sure if they were homeless, but he left the suitcase near them anyway.

When he got outside the building, he saw Abby talking to a man, leaning against a car. "Eric, this man speaks a little English and he said he would drive us to the train station."

Eric got out his wallet and held out what he felt was a fair price and the man nodded and took it. They got in his car and the man started driving. It was an extremely slow process. "I'm beginning to wonder if it wouldn't be faster to walk," Eric said, "but at least we're warm right now."

"I don't understand why Luka doesn't answer you. I know things in Kyiv are worse than here, but he does have some responsibility for us."

"Mom, drop it," Eric sighed. "We haven't a clue of what has happened to Luka. Stop making him a scapegoat."

Abby frowned. "Well, okay then. I guess we'll get to the train station on our own, at least." She looked out the window at all the cars and people. "Eventually."

"It's strange," Eric mused, watching the crowd. "Lines of people trying to get out of here and others just going about their business."

"Maybe the people fleeing are from the parts of the country that are being attacked," Abby replied. "The local residents haven't seen the war firsthand."

"And they don't have relatives in the U.S. feeding them news reports," Eric added.

"They also have a president who is minimizing the danger."

"Do you think Zelensky is still minimizing it?"

Abby shrugged. "Let's ask this driver. Excuse me. Are you going to the train station to leave Ukraine?"

The man shook his head. "Just take you."

"Are you afraid of Russia?" she asked.

He shook his head again. "Always saying they attack. Many years they say that."

"But this time they really are."

He shrugged. "We okay here."

Abby and Eric glanced at each other. They were beginning to understand a little. "There is always a threat, so it's easier not to take it seriously," Abby murmured. "Maybe the Ukrainians are right and the Americans are making a bigger deal out of this. And maybe being in Lviv is okay and that's why Luka isn't worried about us as much as himself and his clients that are still in Kyiv."

"Wishful thinking on his part," Eric replied, "but we might as well join in and think positively."

"What other choice do we have but to think positively?" Abby demanded. "We don't know what's going to happen when we get to the train station. Maybe they won't let us on because Jillian doesn't have a passport. Or maybe because they are giving priority to Ukrainians."

"So much for positive thinking," Eric muttered.

19

AFTER MORE THAN AN HOUR, BUT ONLY A FEW KILOMETERS DISTANCE, TRAFFIC CAME TO A COMPLETE STANDSTILL. "Is the train station close enough to walk from here?" Eric asked the driver.

The man pointed to the left. "Not far."

"Thank you," Abby said as she opened the door and reached in for the car seat.

Eric got out with the suitcase full of Jillian's things and his backpack. "Why don't I take the car seat and you take this suitcase. It's on rollers and will be easier for you to handle. And I'm taller and can hold the car seat higher so as not to bang it against other people."

They switched items and joined the crowd walking to the station. Besides the temperature being freezing, the streets were icy. Abby was glad she didn't have the car seat in her hand as she walked gingerly, remembering too well her fall in the airport. "It's mostly women and children here," she said as she looked around her.

"Probably most of the men are staying to fight," Eric replied. "Remember what that boy said about his father staying behind."

"Yes. I think I read that all men between eighteen and sixty are forbidden to leave. They have to join the military."

"So that would be me," Eric said.

"Well you're not Ukrainian, thank goodness. We baby boomers went through that during the Vietnam War. But there was a draft. Here it seems everyone has to do it."

As they neared the train station, the line became unruly as people pushed and shoved trying to get on the first train. And then the line came to an abrupt halt. "What if we can't get on a train?" Abby moaned. "Then what will we do?"

"Maybe Luka can get us a driver to the Polish border," Eric replied half-heartedly.

"I've given up on him," Abby said sourly. "What does he know about what's going on here in Lviv anyway?"

"It's worth a try," Eric sighed. He texted Luka but he didn't answer. He left a voicemail and looked around for people who looked like they might be police or train station employees. And then Jillian started to cry.

"Oh dear!" Abby lamented. "She's hungry and needs a diaper change." She looked frantically around the impenetrable mass of refugees. "How in the world will we change her diaper? We can't even get inside the train station, no less get on a train!"

Eric's phone rang. It was Luka, starting with a long, apologetic explanation. Eric cut him short and explained their own dilemma, Jillian's complaints adding emphasis. Eric listened for a moment, thanked him and hung up. "He's going to try to find a car and driver for us," Eric reported to Abby. "Fingers crossed."

"Can't," Abby replied, juggling a squalling Jillian, now red-faced with snot running out of her nose. The only plus side was that people were now trying to stay away from them, and through a small gap in the mass of humanity, Abby could see a low wall ahead. It was crowded with older women trying to rest their feet, but as she pushed close, one old woman noticed her and got up. This woman then turned to the woman next to her and started scolding her, and that woman reluctantly rose and moved away. The old lady waved Abby over and started chattering and then realizing the language barrier, started gesticulating and then finally held her nose with a laugh. Somehow in all this chaos, Abby managed to laugh too. The little round woman cupped her wrinkled hands on top of the stone wall, indicating that she would protect Jillian's head if Abby would lay her down to change her. Abby nodded and proceeded to change Jillian's diaper as the old lady cooed and otherwise distracted Jillian.

Abby rolled up the soiled wipes in the dirty diaper and taped it shut, but didn't have a clue how to dispose of it. There was no way to wander off looking for a trashcan, which would be overflowing anyway. The old lady realized the predicament and shrugged, motioning Abby to put it behind the wall. It was then that Abby noticed all the unmentionable waste there, and with a shudder, she dropped the diaper into the mess. Abby picked up Jillian, who was now in a better if not perfect mood, and the old lady kissed her own finger and then touched Jillian's forehead with it. The two women looked at one another for a moment, their eyes bright with unshed tears. Then Abby became aware of Eric talking into his phone behind her.

"Yurus?" Eric repeated. Abby turned and Eric repeated again, looking at her. "Yurus Hostel?"

Abby glanced back at the old lady who shook her head and then settled back onto the wall. The magic moment had passed. Eric raised his voice. "Yurus Hostel!" he frantically repeated. People turned and stared, and finally someone parroted him, pointing in a certain direction. Soon two or three more arms pointed out the same way. Without a word, Abby and Eric gathered all their stuff and pushed ahead.

"Luka found us a driver," Eric explained as they wormed their way through the crowd. "He'll meet us at Yurus Hostel."

"Thank God!" Abby cried.

They struggled through the mass of people, going against the tide, and finally got to the Yurus Hostel. As soon as they walked inside, a woman at the front desk started speaking to them in Ukrainian. "Do you speak English?" Eric asked. She went into a back office and returned with another woman.

"We have no rooms," the new woman said.

"That's okay. A ride is picking us up here. Can we wait in the lobby?"

"You American?"

"Yes."

"Baby born here?"

"Yes."

"Okay." Without further ado, she turned and started walking away.

"Wait!" Eric called out. "Can you warm a bottle for us?" The woman gave him a blank look, so Eric fished out a bottle from the bag and waved it in the air. The woman frowned but waited for him to fill it and then took it. Abby and Eric found a worn sofa in the corner of the lobby and plopped down onto it, raising a cloud of dust. After a few minutes the woman returned and with a more genial expression, handed over the warm bottle of formula. Eric handed Jillian over to Abby. "Please feed her. I want to wait outside for the driver so we don't miss him."

Abby fed Jillian and texted Brian to update him on what was happening. "Thank God you are leaving Ukraine!" he texted back.

"Mom! The driver's here!" Eric called from the doorway.

"Okay, be right there." Abby put Jillian back in her car seat, put her phone back in her purse and hurried outside. They got in the car and the driver squeezed into the crawl of traffic. "Does the driver speak English?" she asked Eric.

"A little bit."

Abby raised her voice. "Thank you so much for picking us up!" The driver didn't answer, but nodded that he understood. Abby thought he was not too happy about driving them to the Polish border except for the large amount of money he expected in return.

Jillian settled into sleeping mode and Abby and Eric both realized they needed to join her while they had a chance. They had no idea what awaited them at the border. They did fall asleep, but not for long. They were startled awake by the sound of the driver's phone ringing and he answered on speaker. A woman's voice was speaking Ukrainian fast and loud. The driver took it off speaker and yelled back into the phone. "Maybe his wife isn't too happy about him taking us," Eric whispered to Abby.

"I don't blame her. He's taking us to the border and not his family."

The slow line of cars had come to a stop and some people started getting out. "Where are we?" Eric asked the driver.

"Bartativ," the driver replied.

"How much further to the Polish border?" The driver shrugged. Eric looked out the back window. "Look at all these cars." He sighed and took out his phone and put Bartativ into the map app. Then he looked for a Polish city closest to the border and mapped the distance to Medyka. "The map says it's forty-two miles to the closest city to the border and it would take a little over an hour."

"And how long will it take if the car stands still?" Abby quipped. Just then the line started inching forward again. Eric and Abby glanced at each other with relief.

But their relief didn't last long when once again the line stopped and the driver's phone rang again. This time he didn't put it on speaker, but Abby and Eric could still hear the woman's voice on the other end, screaming and crying. The driver finally spoke quietly into the phone and hung up. He turned around and said, "Sorry. I go home. Family need me."

Abby sighed and Eric replied, "We understand. I think it's about thirty miles—uh, about fifty kilometers—to the border. Would we stay on this road to walk there?"

The driver grimaced. "It cold for baby."

"I know," Eric answered. "But do we turn off this road or anything if we walk?"

"Stay on road." The driver shook his head. "I sorry."

Abby looked out the window at the line of cars while Eric opened the door. "Wait. Let's at least change her diaper and give her a bottle before we head out in the cold. Who knows when we'll get another chance," Abby said as she took Jillian out of the car seat. "And I think we should ditch the car seat. It would be easier and we could keep her warmer as we walk if we hold her."

"You're right." Eric opened Jillian's suitcase and took out a diaper and a bottle. "Are we going to feed it to her cold?"

"We don't have a choice," Abby replied. "At least it's already mixed."

"Do you mind if we give the baby a bottle first?" Eric asked the driver.

"No . . . no. Do that."

"He feels so bad," Abby whispered to Eric. They changed Jillian and gave her a bottle. "Well, here goes." Abby opened the door and got out with her purse. "Should I carry Jillian or pull her suitcase?"

Eric put on his backpack. "I'll take Jillian and put her under my jacket." He smiled. "You wouldn't want to keep yours open."

"You're right about that. After we're walking a while I'll be warmer and I can hold her." Abby took out the suitcase, Eric paid the driver and wrapped his jacket around Jillian and they were off.

They walked for a while and found many other people had the same idea. There were many children, but no other tiny babies. There was a light snowfall as seemed always to be the case in Ukraine. "Maybe you should carry Jillian now," Eric said as he saw Abby struggling to pull the suitcase on the snow-covered road. They switched the baby for the suitcase and Eric wound up holding it by the handles. "It's easier this way, but it would have been heavy for you."

"So how long do you think it's going to take us to walk thirty miles?" Abby asked.

Eric shrugged. "Don't they say most people walk three to four miles an hour?"

"I think so," Abby responded. "That would be at least eight hours. I guess that's doable."

"It's going to have to be," Eric muttered. "It's not like we have a choice."

The crowd swelled as they trudged along. "It'll take way more than eight hours at this speed," Abby grumbled. She noticed some people stopping and resting on their suitcases, but it didn't seem to thin out the crowd walking. And of course, Jillian started to cry. Abby tried to soothe her, but the more she tried, the louder the baby wailed. "Maybe we need to stop," she called out to Eric.

Eric put the suitcase down and took Jillian from Abby while Abby sat on top of the suitcase. "It's been too long since she was fed," he said.

Abby looked at her watch. "I don't think it's been that long. I wonder what's wrong."

"Hmm," Eric quipped. "She's three weeks old and outside in freezing temperatures?"

"Well, maybe something else is wrong."

"Wouldn't you like to be crying right now too?"

"Yes," Abby nodded.

Just then a woman came over to Eric holding something in her outstretched hand. For a moment Eric flinched, then he saw she was holding a pacifier. Eric and Abby looked at each other. Would it be clean? Was this a good idea during this Covid pandemic to put something in her mouth that they didn't know where it's been? The woman was insistent. She spoke in Ukrainian and Eric put up his finger as if to stay wait a minute. He handed Jillian to Abby and took out his phone. He pressed the translator app and the woman spoke again into the phone. The app then said in English that it was an extra one and it was clean. Eric took it and handed it to Abby who put it in Jillian's mouth and the crying stopped. "Thank you!" Eric said.

The woman smiled and nodded, and returned to her own two children including a toddler with a pacifier in his mouth. "Do you have a pacifier in the suitcase?" Abby asked.

"Yes. Just didn't think of it."

"Maybe you should give her yours. Maybe she needs the extra one."

"I think that would lessen the beautiful thing she just did."

"You're right. Maybe we can pass along the favor later." Abby took a deep breath. "Shall we continue on?"

"Are you ready?" Eric asked.

"As ready as I'll ever be." She put Jillian back under her coat and got off the suitcase so Eric could pick it up. And they continued their trek.

They walked for another hour or so before taking another short break. Eric took out one of the bottles of water he had packed in his backpack and handed it to Abby. "Shouldn't we save these to mix with the dry formula after we run out of the bottled formula?" she asked.

"I think we'll be okay. There are gas stations along the route where we can buy water."

Abby gestured with her arm to the swarms of people around them. "And you think there will be water left in a store on this route?"

Eric shrugged. "Just take a sip or two then, I guess."

Abby took a couple of sips and handed back the bottle. Then she hugged herself to keep warm. "We need to find someplace inside, Eric. It's getting dark and even colder."

Eric peered down the road in gathering twilight. "I think there actually is a gas station ahead."

"Sounds inviting," Abby replied drolly.

They tried to speed up their walking, but then they started having to dodge the crowd, which thwarted any additional forward progress. The quick shifts in their movements disturbed Jillian and she started crying. Like an emergency siren, her cries did have some effect, though as the refugees tended to move aside. They finally felt they were making some real progress.

As they approached the gas station, unsurprisingly teeming with people, they noticed a couple of young men in uniform. They weren't sure if the men were soldiers or police, but Abby went up to them and pointed to Jillian. "We need to get her inside someplace warm." She then pointed to the gas station.

Although they may not have spoken English, they understood what was needed and they made a path through the crowd. Eric and Abby were able to walk briskly and join the wall-to-wall people inside the tiny store There wasn't anything useful left to buy, but it felt good to be warm—even if most of the warmth was from other human bodies.

"Not everyone is wearing a mask," Abby noticed. "And these close quarters . . ."

"Well, we are and it's all we can do."

"But Jillian is not."

Eric sighed. "Then let's use the restroom, change and feed Jillian, and get back on the road."

"It's dark and freezing. Maybe there's a hotel somewhere close?"

"Mom, even if there was a hotel nearby, we'd be lucky to sleep on the lobby floor," snapped Eric. "Not exactly sanitary. I think we only have about twelve miles to the border. We could be there in four hours maybe."

"Eric! We can't walk with a newborn baby for four hours in the middle of the night!"

Several people turned to Abby's shrill voice and Eric bowed his head in embarrassment. "Maybe we should have stayed in Lviv," he murmured.

"Well, that's just a fine and dandy thought," Abby snapped back. Then she too noticed the attention she was drawing and lowered her voice. "We've done our best with no advice and no direction and there's nothing we can do about it except keep Jillian warm. Let's just stay inside here until daylight."

"Mom, just a minute ago you were all worried about Covid and—" the look on his mother's face said don't go there. "Okay, okay. Let's force our way into some spot where we can at least sit down against a wall or something." Using Jillian as some sort of talisman, they managed to secure a spot on the solid end of a display case. Eric texted Luka their situation, but realized any rescue at this point was unlikely due to the jammed roads. Then he leaned into his mother, Jillian settled against his chest, and somehow all three found sleep out of sheer exhaustion.

20

JILLIAN'S WHIMPERING WOKE THEM. It was just getting light outside, so they moved quickly to get the baby changed and fed. Seeing that the shelves around them were empty, Eric pawed through their bag and found a bag of cookies. Without thinking of their suitability for breakfast, he tore open the bag and stuffed one in his mouth, then offered Abby some. She gingerly started eating one and soon another. Eric grinned at her and asked, "When was the last time you had cookies for breakfast?"

"Oh I don't know," she laughed. "Maybe sixty years ago! I don't know if it's the sleep, or the sugar is already kicking in, or knowing that we may actually be at the border in four hours, but I do feel energized." She glanced around at the cars at a standstill. "Although I've been bitching about the cold, it's probably best that the driver left to go home. We'd still be days away from the border if we'd stayed in the car."

Eric's phone dinged twice. One message was from Heather, asking if they'd gotten to the border yet. And the other one was from Luka. He apologized, but didn't know what he could do to help them until they got to the border. He said he had called the embassy in Poland to alert them that you would be arriving without a passport for Jillian. Eric filled Abby in on what Luka had said. "I wonder if someone from the embassy will actually be at the border waiting for us," he mused.

"Don't count on it," Abby scoffed. "But there should be someone at the border who can help us."

"I'm going to try and call Heather while we walk and see if she's heard anything about the war and the border crossing on American news." He tried to call, but he only got a recording in Ukrainian.

"There will probably be relief workers at the border," Abby mused. "All these people trying to get into Poland . . . there has to be some concerted effort from Poland, if not from America and other countries, to help."

"We'll see," Eric replied half-heartedly. They walked on and the closer they got to the border, the more crowded it got. "I wish we could find out what's going—" His sentence was flattened by a huge explosion. People screamed and started running in every direction.

Abby grabbed Eric and clung to him. "Oh my God! Are they bombing us now?!" She looked around frantically as Jillian started screaming. "What'll we do?"

"I don't know." Eric put his arm around her and she could feel her heart race. "I don't see any safe place nearby to run to."

"Well, they're running," Abby cried, jutting her chin out at the crowd around them.

"Yeah, but where? They're just running scared."

Abby choked back a sob and tightened her hold on Jillian. She glanced at her Fitbit. "I think we only have two or three miles left."

"Then let's just keep walking," Eric's voice cracked. He tried Heather again, and this time the call went through. "We're only a few miles from the border. What does the news say now about what's going on here?" He turned to Abby repeating what Heather was telling him on the phone. "Still bombing in the south and east. The area around Kyiv is getting hit too."

"Ask her if she has heard anything about the western border."

Eric asked and then shook his head to Abby. "Jillian's fine," he smiled. "A real trooper." And then there was another loud explosion. "I don't know what that was," he yelled into the phone, "but I'd better go now." He ended the call before Heather could react and stared at his mother's imploring look. Unnerved, he turned away to gaze at the horizon. "I think that's too far away to really worry about," he said, looking back at her. "Let's just plow ahead. We could be at the border in an hour."

Abby sighed and nodded. They continued walking, the refugees pressing closer and closer together. "Where are all these people coming from?" she asked.

"Everywhere," Eric replied. "There can't be many border crossings in a time of war, so all roads lead here." He looked down at Jillian who regarded the growing crowd warily. "She's been so quiet," he murmured. "I almost think she just knows that she needs to chill." As if to prove otherwise, Jillian let out a wail of protest.

"We're almost there, sweet baby," Abby said soothingly, pulling Jillian away from her body and rocking her gently. After a few seconds she looked up again and found that Eric had been swallowed by the mob around them. She panicked. "Eric! Eric!"

"Mom?" he shouted back. He looked around, but he kept getting pushed further and further away from where they had been standing together by the sea of people.

"Eric!!!" Abby screamed, but her voice was drowned out by the roar of the crowd. In this pure desperation she was no longer given any courtesy that carrying Jillian had offered, but was being elbowed and jostled just like everyone else. Jillian was screaming too—but so were countless other children and babies. She tried to stand her ground, but felt like she was being pushed back. She could not wait for Eric to find her. It was imperative that she get to the border where there would be guards and soldiers and with any luck maybe even someone from the American embassy. She started pushing forward and hoped Eric would do the same.

Eric was frantic as well, but he felt that it was more important to find Abby and Jillian, so he tried to get back to where he had left them. He finally got to where he thought they separated, but, of course, his mother and his daughter were nowhere to be seen. He then started in the direction of the border, trying to maneuver with his backpack and the suitcase full of Jillian's things. It was slow going.

Abby, meanwhile, having been born and raised in Manhattan, knew how to shove her way through a crowd. She started pushing harder, but no one was giving her an inch. She started to worry about Jillian being smothered, but at least her cries let Abby know she could breathe. Tears of frustration rolled down Abby's face as she pleaded, prodded and cursed her way forward when suddenly she felt a strong tug at her elbow. Someone was trying to pull her aside. "NO!" she screamed. "What are you trying to do to me?!" She pulled away, but suddenly the rest of the person appeared, a woman with a plaintive smile and a teenage girl at her side.

The woman held tight and nudged the girl who then said, "We help you." The woman started pulling again and Abby was reluctantly dragged to the other side of the road. Here a man in uniform stood, ignoring the pleas and threats of the refugees around him. He did seem to come to his senses, however, when they appeared and the woman began speaking rapidly in Ukrainian, with the girl adding "American!" for emphasis. The man nodded and said a few words and reached out to escort Abby as the girl said, "He take you now." The crowd grew more unruly as they saw what they thought was some sort of preferential treatment, but he plowed ahead and she followed in his wake. Abby turned back to see the woman and girl timidly waving, and she wiped the tears out of her eyes and blew them a kiss back.

Abby's anxiety dropped a notch as she followed in the wake of the uniformed man. Even Jillian seemed to sense some sort of relief, as her protests fell to soft cries. The crowd filled in behind them, eager for any forward movement, only to thwart themselves by their own gridlock of bodies. Abby thought of how to present their case and then remembered Eric had the bottle, the formula and the diapers—she wouldn't have much time before Jillian would have a meltdown. Suddenly they were at a gate and her mind was blank. The uniformed man spoke to a guard who then disappeared for a while. He returned with another guard. "Passport?" the new guard asked.

"I'm American and—"

"I know. Passport." Abby rummaged through her purse, which wasn't an easy task while holding a screaming infant. She finally found it and handed it over. He gave it a lookover and held on to it. "And baby?"

"I-I don't have a passport for the baby. The embassy closed and then the war started and we——"

"Birth certificate," he interrupted impatiently.

"Oh-h-h, my son has it, but we got separated in the crowd."

The guard's eyes narrowed. "Your son?"

"Yes." Suddenly a cascade of facts fell through her mind, such as that Eric didn't have the same last name as her due to her second marriage. She felt untethered—unhinged, really—while fully aware that the guard was studying her for false pretense. "Oh! How stupid of me!" she blurted out. "I'll call him!" Jillian cranked up the screaming as she again rummaged through her purse and then she finally found her phone. She pressed the screen and flashed the guard a fake, frightened smile. The call went to voicemail. "Eric! Oh God, Eric! I'm at the border gate! Where are you?" She ended the call and again flashed that smile. "He didn't answer. He probably didn't hear it ring, you know. He'll call me back soon, I'm sure."

"I'm sure," mimicked the guard. "You're American. Why you in Ukraine?"

"Well," she faltered. How much would he let her explain? "The baby was born here and—"

"Son not Ukrainian?"

"No, no! Born in America, like me. No draft dodger! We're bringing the baby home to America."

"Oh, you adopt." It was clear he was looking for a reaction. Abby pondered whether she should bother to correct him, but was afraid if she didn't, that he would think she was a liar. And then what would happen? Her phone started ringing as she thought out her strategy. "You answer," the guard said, pointing to the phone clutched in her hand.

"Oh!" she laughed nervously. "It's Eric." She put it on speakerphone. "Eric! Where are you?!"

"I don't know, but I can't be far from the gate. Don't move!"

"I don't think I can," she laughed again, glancing at the guard.

"What?"

"Nothing, nothing. We'll be here, God willing." She ended the call. "See?" she told the guard. "He should be here soon with the birth certificate."

The guard's demeanor softened slightly. "I hope so."

With some of the pressure off, Abby was suddenly chilled. "Is there someplace close by where we can warm up?" she ventured. "The baby is only three weeks old."

"No," he replied firmly. But he did start looking around, finally picking out a young man and speaking sharply to him in Ukrainian. The young man was clearly dismayed, but responded to another barked order by peeling off his jacket.

"Oh, I couldn't," Abby protested.

"You must. For baby." The guard tented the jacket over Jillian and Abby's shoulders, tying the arms around her neck to hold it in place. It smelled of sweat and Abby was sure the guard was using it to muffle Jillian as much as to offer some warmth.

Meanwhile, Eric was getting nowhere fast. A step forward, a step aside, a shove back. He wished he had Jillian to clear the way, but then doubted her magic would work anymore. He could hear screaming babies, crying children. The suitcase full of Jillian's supplies slipped from his grasp. He whirled around, only to find it disappear into the chaos. He couldn't waste time looking for it. He patted his jacket, assuring himself that all the documents were on him, and again pressed forward. If he could only make them understand that he didn't belong there—that he was American. Finally, out of sheer desperation, he started shouting, "American! American!" Laughter and jeering erupted around him and he was shoved aside. He stumbled and almost fell, and the fear of being trampled overwhelmed him. He hunched down and fairly cannonballed in no particular direction, just to find some breathing space, as he perceived the crowd turning on him. He went headlong into the chain link fence, which seemed to delight the few that actually saw it happen. He splayed his fingers, grabbing the link so he wouldn't fully sink to the ground.

Surely it wasn't the springy sound of a body hitting the fence that caught Abby's attention. Not with the roar of the refugees. No. Some sort of maternal instinct pricked her shivering body, and she peered far down the fence. Plenty of objects were being pushed through the links—

futile bribes of cash, watches and jewelry. Fingers fluttered, fists pulled inward on the links—but only one pair of hands clung there. At that moment, his mother saw him.

"Eric!" Abby screamed, brushing past the guard. She pulled Jillian tight against her body and started running along the inside of the fence. The guard followed her and was joined by other guards on her heels. "Eric!" Adrenaline catapulted her forward, just out of reach of the guards that kept grabbing at her. In an instant she was stumbling to a stop along the fence where Eric slowly raised himself. The guards grabbed her, crushing Jillian against her chest. "Stop! Let me go! It's my son!"

"Momma!" Abby hadn't heard that in over thirty-five years—and she burst into tears.

"Show them her birth certificate!" Abby cried above Jillian's piercing screams.

Eric fished the paper out of the inside of his jacket, rolled it up and pushed it through the fence. The guard who had been standing with Abby grabbed it and studied it for a moment. "Passport!" he demanded. Eric fished through the other side of his jacket, pulled it out and bent it to force it through the links. Again the guard studied. "Last name not same."

"I remarried!" screamed Abby. "He's my son!"

The guard compared the two passports. "Both California," he finally said.

"Yes!" cried Eric.

"Warm there . . ." murmured the guard.

"Yes—" Abby wanted to laugh, but was too exhausted. Suddenly Jillian felt like she weighed two hundred pounds, and it seemed like one of the secondary guards was holding her up. The top guard closed the two passports and put them in one of his pockets and yelled some sort of order in Ukrainian. The other guards just looked at him, and so he motioned with the rolled birth certificate that Eric was somehow to be escorted to the gate.

The crowd pushed forward, eager for any remote chance of entry. The guards yelled toward the fence, temporarily causing the refugees to back off and make a small path for Eric to move toward the gate. When Abby tried to follow on the other side she almost collapsed. A young guard snatched Jillian, now purple with rage, from her arms and the head guard grabbed her around the waist, half dragging her slowly along. Eric called out assurances to Jillian as he inched along, and she, now held in the open, started returning to a healthier color and demeanor. She kept her eyes glued to her daddy on the other side of the fence. They all inched along, allowing Abby to recover somewhat by the time they reached the gate. Eric slipped through and grabbed his mother. "You were fantastic," he murmured. "A lioness."

"An *old* lioness," Abby groaned.

Eric kissed her on the forehead. "No matter."

The head guard touched her elbow. "Just some emergency paperwork to do," he said. "Red Cross nearby."

"Oh thank God! Jillian needs—well everything," sighed Abby, pulling away from Eric.

The young guard held out the now rank smelling baby, who had pretty much exhausted herself into a state of stupor. "Phew!" Eric cried, taking Jillian. "Where was Daddy's little stinker when he needed her to clear the way?"

21

THE TINY OFFICE QUICKLY STARTED TO SMELL. Abby sat on a chair in the corner, holding Jillian who was fast asleep, her face crusty from dirt and dried tears. The guard sat at a cluttered desk, and Abby was sure he was rushing through the paperwork just to get them out of there. He scribbled out forms, indicating where Eric was to sign and stamped their passports. Other guards came and went, apparently reporting on various checkpoints and operations.

"Welcome to Poland," the guard said automatically, rising and handing over their paperwork. "You may proceed. But sorry. Red Cross not arrived yet."

"But—" Abby gasped. "The baby needs formula . . . diapers. Everything was in our suitcase . . ."

"Sorry," the guard repeated. "Maybe stroller? Many left nearby."

"I don't think that would help," Eric replied impatiently. "Are there any American embassy workers around?"

"No. I hear no such thing. Go to Warsaw."

"How?"

The guard shrugged. "Bus? Train? Sorry."

Eric looked over at his mother, who bit her lip in an effort not to cry. "Let's go," she choked.

"Let's," he mumbled.

Fortunately Jillian was too exhausted to be disturbed much by their exit. They stood outside, taking deep breaths of cold, fresh air while trying to figure out what to do next. The low gray skies made everything look forbidding, but there were strollers, lined up some distance away. "It's such a nice gesture," Abby murmured. "Lovely, really."

"But a stroller would be awkward once we got transportation," Eric countered. "And we don't have anything to keep Jillian warm in one."

"I know." She stood there watching for a moment. "What are those women doing next to them? They're not even looking at the strollers."

"I don't know, but they have bags of something," Eric replied. "Let's go see what they're doing."

A thin layer of dirty snow scrunched under their feet. When they approached, the women smiled and said obvious greetings, gathering to have a look at Jillian. Once it was clear there was a language barrier, the women simply opened their bags, showing what they had to offer. One woman had an opened box of wipes, which she simply handed over to Eric. Another had some diapers, but they were way too big. Another bag revealed several bottles of formula.

"Oh!" gasped Abby, reaching out with her free hand. The woman closed the bag and made some sort of announcement. The woman who gave away the wipes started scolding her.

"She wants money," Eric said.

"Then give her some!"

Eric reached into his pocket and pulled some out. The woman simply swiped it all and started walking away. "Hey!"

The woman who had given the wipes went on a fresh tirade at the retreating woman while another stepped up and offered a very garish, very small onesie. "We better take that, even if it'll make Jillian look like a clown," Abby said. "The one she has on is filthy and who knows when we can wash it out."

Eric again fished in his pocket, producing some more money. The woman pointed out what seemed like a fair amount. "Ok," Eric nodded, and she took just that.

The last two women also had things, but they were unsuitable for a baby as young as Jillian. "Well, this is a miracle," Abby said as she looked over their finds. "Except for no diapers."

"Maybe we could make one," Eric pondered.

"With what?" Paper napkins?"

The woman who gave them the wipes lingered. She seemed to want to help further. She started pointing and repeating herself.

"Warsaw?" Eric asked. She tilted her head and made a face, as if to say sorta. "Wait!" Eric said. "My translator app." Slowly the app deciphered that there was a bus taking women and children somewhere. Maybe toward Warsaw, "There's a bus going somewhere, so we're not stuck here," Eric said excitedly.

"Let's hope it's going somewhere we want to be, and not some refugee camp."

"At least a camp would likely have diapers."

"True," sighed Abby.

The woman pointed again, first at herself and then in that certain direction, motioning them to follow. They walked for some time along a narrow road, cars whizzing past them. Eric took over carrying Jillian, but Abby was still frightened she might not make it after all the day's trauma. The sun broke through, causing the shoulder of the road to go soft and slushy, requiring them to put that much more effort into the journey. After taking a short rest they eventually came to a crossroads that had a convenience store of sorts, where a group of women and children milled about. There was a folding table with bottled water on it and a large pile of stale plain rolls, and upon seeing new arrivals someone in charge discreetly gave them each what looked like a protein bar, Eric went into the store and triumphantly returned. "Diapers!" he announced, producing a small package like it was a tiara on a velvet pillow.

"Thank God!" exclaimed Abby, dropping her bags of baby goods. "Let the excavation begin!"

The woman cleared a bench of weary refugees and helped Abby clean up Jillian as best they could. Then they put her in the newly acquired onesies, and Jillian even cracked a smile. "She likes being a court jester," Eric laughed, picking her up. "Time to feed her."

"Go easy," Abby warned. "She hasn't had anything for ages and all that excitement." The woman gave Abby her protein bar, gathered up several rolls and bid them goodbye. Eric made sure to use the app to express their extreme gratitude. The woman's cheeks grew rosier and then she turned and started back to where she came from. "An absolute angel," Abby murmured as she watched her disappear.

"Yes," Eric agreed, looking up momentarily from Jillian's calculated feeding.

Soon some sort of announcement was made and all the women and children started gathering up their belongings and stuffing rolls into anything that would hold them, including the hands of the children. Abby stuffed a couple more into her purse and then picked up Jillian. "This is going to be interesting," Eric said, once again feeling his jacket for his passport and birth certificate.

"What?"

"Well, I'm the only guy here. Even the driver is a woman. What if she doesn't let me on?"

"You're Jillian's father."

"And none of these kids have fathers?"

"Well, of course they do—and you have the birth certificate, border crossing papers and an American passport. Relax."

Eric frowned and looked back at the authoritative looking driver. "Can I borrow your lipstick?"

"No," Abby deadpanned. "Besides, I haven't seen it for days."

Eric rubbed his whiskers as he approached the door. Unsurprisingly the driver would not let him on. He produced his paperwork and used the app as she passively let the others board. Abby found a seat near the door and then leaned out the window to add her two unintelligible cents to the largely pantomimed argument. To everyone's surprise, there were a few seats left after everyone got on. The driver looked around, gave a sharp whistle, looked around again, and finally let Eric board with a curt flip of her head.

The situation had garnered a lot of curiosity from the other riders, so the seat next to Abby stayed safely unoccupied. Eric sat down and took Jillian, resuming a careful feeding. She was hungry, but also tired—at any rate, not as demanding as he expected and her eyes started to droop as he talked to her. The mothers and children around him watched longingly, missing their husbands and fathers. Soon Jillian fell asleep, and not long after, so did Eric. As his grip loosened on her, Abby took the bottle and gently lifted Jillian onto her chest. She felt a sense of serenity she hadn't felt in ages. Maybe they'd make it home after all.

They rode for a couple of hours, although not as far as one would assume in that period of time. Traffic was heavy, but nothing like it had been in Ukraine. Occasionally the driver took side roads that didn't seem to do much good except relieve the eye of the long exodus ahead of them on the highway. Eventually the bus came to a stop at a petrol station and the driver made an announcement. Abby presumed it was a rest stop, but everyone started to collect their belongings. Abby shook Eric's shoulder. "Eric—I think we have to get off here."

Eric rubbed his eyes and yawned. "Where are we?"

"I don't know. At a gas station somewhere. People are taking their stuff and leaving."

"Well, I guess we'll have to do the same," he sighed. He wearily stood up and took his backpack off the overhead shelf. Abby followed Eric off the bus carrying Jillian, now awake and starting to whimper.

22

'I'LL BE SURPRISED IF WE DON'T GET COVID," ABBY SCOFFED AS SHE PLUCKED AT HER MASK TO GET A BREATH OF FRESH AIR. "This one feels like a junior science project."

"Thanks for the reminder, Mom," Eric drawled. "Like we don't have enough to worry about." He scanned the scene outside the bus. There already appeared to be a line for the restroom at the gas station, and maybe there was a town over that-a-way.

"Do you want a new one?" Abby asked. "I think I have a few left in my purse."

"I'm sure they're sparkly clean way down there with your car keys and gum wrappers."

"Why would I have my car keys?!" demanded Abby. "I cleaned out my purse before leaving. And I don't chew gum!"

"A lot has happened in there since you cleaned out your purse."

"Tell me about it," she sighed. "Well, *I* want a *cleaner* mask," she announced, holding out Jillian.

Eric took Jillian and Abby starting rummaging through her purse, eventually producing two masks. She reached one out to Eric. "Keep mine for close quarters, please," he said.

"I can't think of anything closer than waiting in line for the restroom."

"Ah, but I'm a guy. I can just go around–—"

"Not with Jillian in one arm!" snapped Abby. "And I need to get in line."

"Okay," Eric replied meekly. "Maybe I'll call the American Embassy while I wait."

"With a baby in your arms . . ."

"Mom, I've been a father before. Remember?"

"Yes," Abby replied, biting her lip. "Sorry."

Abby got in line and Eric wandered about until finding a bench to sit on. There were already several women there, but they moved down to make room for him at the very end. With Jillian in his lap and held by the crook of his arm, he started searching for a phone number. It took some earnest explanation to get through reception, but soon he was pleasantly surprised to find himself talking to someone who seemed to actually be interested in helping. "Where are you exactly?" the woman asked.

"I-I don't know. The border crossing was crazy and we hopped on the first bus that would take us away from there."

"And you're on a cell phone?"

"Yes."

"And you have a map app?"

"Yes! How stupid of me. My brain has fogged over."

"Understandably," the woman replied sympathetically. "Just see if you can get me a town you're at."

Eric switched to speakerphone, opened the map, and started zooming in and out. "Looks like Route 94 east of Rzeszow."

"Okay." He could hear her typing. "Let me start with investigating some transportation options. Your number?" Eric gave it. "Good, that's a match to what's on my screen. I'll call you back when I have more information. Don't leave the area unless absolutely necessary."

"We won't. I haven't heard anything this good in days. Thank you so much." Eric ended the call and cuddled Jillian. "Grandma will be back soon—and then we'll change and feed you."

Eventually Abby returned. "You're lucky you're a man."

"It comes in handy."

Abby gave him a deadly look and handed over some chips and chocolate bars. "Our health kick continues. Did you get through to the embassy?"

"Yes. They'll get back to us with some transportation options."

"I'd settle for a mule," Abby sighed.

"What? And have to deal with another ass?"

Abby chuckled. "Let's get the little girl cleaned up and fed." They hoped they'd get a return call within minutes, but after a while the cold made them retreat to the gas station. The little shop was crowded and noisy, but Jillian slept right through it. Hours passed. "My legs are going numb," Abby finally said, shifting her weight from one leg to another. "Maybe you should call them again."

"We're not the only Americans in this predicament. I don't want to pester them."

"Maybe we're not the only Americans to escape from Ukraine, but I doubt there are many with a newborn. You did tell her we have a three-week-old baby, didn't you?"

"Of course I did," Eric answered irritably. "I told her our whole story."

"Are we in the same time zone as Lviv?" she asked, looking at her Fitbit. "I'm afraid the embassy might close soon."

"I'm sure she's doing her best and will call." He poked at his phone. "And yes, we are in the same time zone and so is Warsaw."

"Well, it's four o'clock."

Eric sighed. "I'll wait until four-thirty. I'm going to take Jillian outside for a short walk."

"I'll stay here with your backpack. It's too cold out there anyway."

The crowd had thinned considerably as people left to walk or be picked up. Eric watched as a few cars arrived and Ukrainians piled into them. He wondered who was driving the cars. Were they Poles who knew the people they were picking up? Perhaps there were car services being called? He got back inside and told Abby what he had seen.

"Maybe Uber is coming here," she wondered.

Just then Eric's phone rang and he answered excitedly. "Okay. Yes—that's where we are. We'll be here waiting. Thank you so much." He hung up and grinned. "Someone is coming to get us and bring us to the train station in Rzeszow. Then we get a train to Warsaw."

"Did she say how long before someone gets here?"

"About an hour."

"And how far is Rzeszow?"

Eric looked at his map. "About an hour."

"Will there be a train when we get there?"

"I don't know."

"Maybe we should get a hotel room in Rzeszow and then get on a train tomorrow to Warsaw."

"One step at a time," Eric replied. "I was thinking. Maybe we can offer the driver extra money and he can drive us all the way to Warsaw."

"That's a great idea. We could get a hotel in Warsaw and then deal with the embassy and planes back to the U.S."

"I'll try."

The driver arrived about two hours later, enough time to feed and change Jillian one more time. "She's certainly cleaner than we are," Abby muttered as she climbed into the car.

"A shower would be nice," Eric sighed blissfully.

"I know. Well, Jillian will have quite a story to tell when she's older."

"You better write it down for her."

"Oh, I will. She's been amazing! Such a good baby!"

Eric leaned toward the driver. "Do you speak English?"

"A little."

Abby and Eric looked at each other with relief. "Would you be willing to take us to Warsaw if we pay you extra?"

"How much?"

"You tell me. How much would you want?"

The driver paused and stopped the car. He turned around and looked at the baby. "You have zloty? Polish money?"

Eric's face fell. He didn't have Polish money, just Ukrainian—and very little left at that. "Oh shit! No, I don't, but I can have my bank send you money. I can give you what's left of our Ukrainian as good faith."

The driver shook his head. "How about American?!" Abby burst out.

"You have one hundred U.S. dollars?" the driver asked.

"Yes!" Abby responded excitedly. She went through a side pocket of her wallet. "My one hundred dollar emergency bill to the rescue!"

The driver took the money and with a bow of his head thanked her. "Where in Warsaw?"

"Any hotel near the embassy," Eric answered.

"I take you to American embassy. They help you."

"But it will be the middle of the night," Abby cut in. "The embassy won't be open."

"That'll be fine. Just take us to the embassy," Eric assured both the driver and Abby. He opened his map app to follow their progress.

The driver nodded and started the car again. He pulled out onto the road and then turned to

Abby, smiling. "Many hotels and restaurants near the embassy."

Abby exhaled loudly. "Oh thank you. We just escaped from Ukraine with this three-week-old baby."

"I was told," he replied, turning back to his driving.

"You're a lifesaver!" Abby could see him grin via the rear view mirror. She sank back against the seat and sighed, letting the stress ooze out of her. Jillian had those sleepy eyes, staring at her Daddy. They finally seemed out of danger. The car moved along steadily, if not quickly.

"I don't think this is going to take just four or five hours," Eric murmured.

"Well, we're in a car at least," Abby replied. "And I doubt all these cars are going to Warsaw. Maybe the road will clear up after we pass through that city where the train station is. What was it called again?"

"Rzeszow."

"Polish doesn't sound any easier than Ukrainian. You'd better switch out your translator app to Polish."

"And probably exchange my few hyrvnia for zloty."

"Look at you remembering the names of all this foreign money!" she laughed.

"It's not hard, Mom."

"Maybe not for forty-year-olds."

Eric grinned and patted her knee. "Thanks for everything. You are the real trooper."

She kissed his cheek. "For you and this darling granddaughter . . . anything."

23

THE CAR CRESTED A HILL AND UP AHEAD WAS THE UNMISTAKABLE FLICKER OF RED POLICE LIGHTS. A long trail of brake lights preceded them, flashing bright and dim as the cars inched along. Abby leaned forward to get a better view from between the front seats. "A wreck?" Eric asked. The driver said nothing and Eric just shrugged.

It was too dark to see anything but the glare of lights on the back of the cars ahead and the headlights of the occasional car that approached. They crept along, a car or two pulling out of the line along the way due to some sort of trouble or need. Jillian sensed Abby's increasing anxiety and her near perfect record of contentment came to an end. "I'd love to join you," Abby said as she tried to comfort the baby. "This is definitely something to scream about." With Eric's help, she got Jillian down to a pattern of wailing as they approached the police cars. The driver spoke to a police officer for some time before the driver told them to show their passports. This seemed to satisfy the policeman and they were allowed to proceed.

"What was that all about?" asked Eric.

"Who we are and where we going."

"That's all?" Abby asked. "Seemed like a lot of conversation."

The driver shrugged. "He say road to Warsaw crowded."

"Did he tell us another way to go?" Eric asked.

"Not his job. Looking for criminals and undocumented entry. He just say take long time. Maybe ten hour."

"Is that okay with you?"

The driver shrugged again. "I stuck now. Maybe more money."

Abby and Eric exchanged knowing looks. If this man was going to squeeze more money out of them, it didn't matter. They had no choice. "We'd save on a hotel, at least," Eric murmured to Abby. "In ten hours the embassy might be open."

The car cruised steadily now, if rarely above sixty kilometers an hour. The gas gauge was getting low, and they passed several closed stations until finding one open. There was a long line waiting at the pumps. "Well, at least it gives us time to use the restrooms and clean up Jillian," sighed Abby. Eric took Jillian so Abby could stand in line.

He wandered around the store, which was not unlike a small truck stop in America. There was even a shelf of baby goods, so he got another small package of diapers and stuffed a couple of bottles of premixed formula in his backpack. Suddenly a clerk appeared, pushing him toward the cashier. "I'm paying for them!" Eric cried out, blushing deeply. "I'm paying!" Everyone in line was staring and talking excitedly.

A man broke from the line and approached him, putting his hand on his shoulder. "Okay," he said, then turned to the clerk and spoke rapidly to her. The woman seemed satisfied and went off in a huff. The man then turned to the line and made some sort of plea, touching Eric's shoulder again. The response was begrudging, but Eric was allowed to cut in line.

"Thank you, " Eric said quietly.

"Okay," the man replied, patting him again. "Okay," he repeated, letting his hand rest on his shoulder. He then leaned toward Jillian, trying to distract her from her soft wailing. Once at the counter the man spoke for him and Eric handed over a credit card, hoping there wouldn't be any glitches. Nearby there was a cold case with a few sandwiches in it He pointed to one and hoped he could salvage half of it for his mother's consumption. The transaction went smoothly and Eric nodded farewell to the man, escaping into the darkness. He found a low wall, leaned back and propped Jillian against his hip as he fumbled with the sandwich packaging. He peeled some sort of meat off one half, piling it on the other, leaving his mother with a cheese sandwich. He stuffed the meaty half in his mouth, feeling hot tears run down his cheeks. Jillian's eyes were bright with reflections from the store, and she watched him intently. Eric felt ashamed yet strangely proud. He stuffed the rest of the sandwich in his mouth and wiped away his tears with the back of his hand.

Abby appeared a few minutes later. He kept his face turned toward the darkness, so she couldn't see his tears. "How goes it?" she asked.

"Well, I almost got arrested for shoplifting, but I got you half a sandwich."

"Oh my God, that's the last thing we need."

"Tell me about it," he muttered, handing her the half a sandwich. "If it wasn't for a good Samaritan who stuck up for me, it could have been ugly."

Abby peeled back the bread to inspect the contents. "Bless them," she sighed, taking a big bite of sandwich. She chewed a little and said with a mouthful, "I don't know what this tastes like, but it's moist and oily. I'm so tired of dry bread and cookies."

Eric got busy changing Jillian's diaper as Abby finished her sandwich. Soon he heard a sharp whistle and saw the driver waving at the far side of the pumps, so he quickly buttoned Jillian's onesie as Abby gathered up the rest of their stuff. Back on the road, the driver sipped from a big cup of coffee while Abby fed Jillian. Eric rummaged through his backpack and Abby's purse, looking for anything else to eat. He gnawed at a roll, pushing it down with bottled water.

"Why don't you give Jillian to me and get some rest," offered Eric.

"I don't think I can. You go first."

"You've got to be exhausted, Mom."

"It's okay. I'd rather you got rest. I may not be able to fall asleep anyway and I'd hate to waste precious time trying when you'd surely utilize it."

Eric shrugged. "Okay." He was asleep in no time and Abby gazed at her son and granddaughter and sighed. She still couldn't believe that this was all happening. A month ago they were worried about a virus that was killing people in record numbers . . . now they were worried about staying warm and finding a way home.

They drove slowly for a couple of hours and Abby thought about trying to engage the driver in some conversation, as she was worried that he'd fall asleep at the wheel. She was enjoying the peace and quiet, however. She could have driven for hours when she was his age. She looked at her phone, thinking she should text Brian, and much to her dismay, it was dead. "Oh no!" she said aloud.

"You okay?" the driver asked.

"I guess, Just that my phone is dead. Not surprised after all this time." She looked around the dashboard, but soon realized the car was too old for a USB port. The cord was probably at the bottom of her purse, anyway . . . hopefully.

"You charge at embassy."

"Yeah. I hate to be without it, though, even for that short time. Funny how things become so necessary." The driver just nodded, as he suddenly seemed to be tackling a rough stretch of road. The car thumped along as he held the wheel at an angle and Abby was quite sure he muttered a cuss word. "What's happening?"

The driver grunted and let the car swerve to the side of the road. Eric woke up at that moment. "Is something wrong?" he asked.

"Something's wrong with the car," Abby explained.

"Flat," announced the driver.

"Do you have a spare tire?" Eric asked. The driver nodded as he grabbed a flashlight out of the glove box. "I'll help you change it. Mom, you'd better get out of the car."

Abby wrapped herself and Jillian in her coat and stepped out. "Damn it's cold!" she exclaimed.

"Changing a tire will warm you up," snorted Eric.

— - -

"Well, it's not *that* cold," Abby replied, snuggling Jillian against her.

The driver was tossing things out of the trunk to get to the spare. He unscrewed the fly nut, listed the spare and let it drop. It was quite obvious by the way it didn't bounce that it was flat. The driver started cursing. "Gotta pump?" Eric said hopefully . . . and desperately. The driver stared at him so Eric motioned using a bicycle pump.

"No!" spit the driver. He fished around in his pocket. "I call." He dialed a number of times, repeating the same sentences as he grew redder in the face. "Busy, busy, busy! No come until morning at least!"

"We'll freeze to death!" Abby cried.

"No we won't," Eric retorted. "We've got plenty of gas."

"We've got to get home!"

Eric didn't stop her from approaching the traffic that was rolling by. Drivers tooted their horn and swerved. "Help us! Help!" Often there was the distinct sound of acceleration as a response to her pleas. Where there were gaps in traffic, she boldly got into the lane and waited for headlights to light up her body. Then she'd flash a view of Jillian before stepping aside. "Help!"

"She craze!" yelped the driver.

"Yeah," gulped Eric. He approached Abby, but she sidestepped to get ahead of him. He decided that trying to pursue her was more dangerous than letting her dance on the side of the road. Minutes passed. "Well, at least she's keeping warm," he muttered. "I'm freezing to death." He turned to see the driver hugging himself. Eric nodded for him to get back into the car and then started to follow suit when he heard car brakes squeal. Fearing the worst, he spun around, but only to see a car roll onto the shoulder and come to a stop ahead of their disabled car. Abby ran toward it, with Eric on her heels, as a man got out.

"Help?" the man asked haltingly.

Abby started spewing her story, but it was clear the man didn't understand anything she was saying. Inside the car were two children, a woman who looked to be in her thirties, and an older woman about Abby's age, blinking at the spectacle before them. Eric waved their driver over and he started explaining the situation. Eric went to his mother, now with tears streaming down her face, and held her. Jillian was in a similar state, sandwiched between them. A minute or two later their driver came over. "They take her and baby. No room for you."

"Oh God—no! Abby blurted out.

"Shhh," Eric soothed. "If you want to get Jillian to the embassy ASAP, this is the way to do it.

"No!"

"I take son to embassy when tire fixed," promised the driver.

"Oh-h-h," Abby sobbed, looking at the passengers staring back at her, wavering, wishing this was just some weird mirage before them. "I don't like it, but I guess I must. But Eric! My phone is dead!"

"Don't worry and don't go anywhere once you get there." Eric was already retreating to the car. He grabbed her purse and quickly sorted out what was absolutely necessary. A few diapers, a few bottles. Her wallet and passport. The birth certificate. Papers from the Polish border. He also left a stale roll inside. Her purse was bulging bigger than ever when he returned. "Here!" Eric was caught off guard by her relative composure. "Everything you need is in here."

Abby swallowed. "Thank you, sweetie." She leaned over, kissed him on the cheek, and then piled into the crowded car. Eric handed her the purse and shut the door. The car rolled away.

"My God . . ." Eric muttered, watching the tail lights dim into the distance.

"Yeah," agreed the driver.

Inside the car, Abby sat stiffly, clutching Jillian. Her purse was a burden on the lap of a wide-eyed boy in the middle. Up front the older woman turned and gave the boy a sympathetic eye. She pointed to Abby, her purse, and then patted her lap.

"Oh," Abby nodded. With a free hand she glanced inside her purse. Her computer and phone, both filled with her contacts, passwords, and personal information would now be in the hands of a complete stranger. Abby nodded and handed her purse over the seat. The woman took it and cradled it as if she understood how important it was to her. Tears started rolling down Abby's cheeks anew, and the woman sitting in the back seat freed the girl's hand from her lap and took hold of Abby's hand. "Thank you," murmured Abby.

Fortunately, Jillian fell asleep after the ordeal, and they rode for a couple of hours in complete silence. When Jillian finally awoke, Abby asked the older woman for a bottle. The woman looked perplexed. Abby imitated holding a bottle over Jillian's mouth and finally the younger woman said something. The older woman opened the purse and found a bottle filled with formula and handed it to Abby. Jillian settled into a feeding and Abby decided not to worry about changing her diaper. A diaper rash was the least of her problems right now, and she wasn't noticing any smell. The few words spoken seemed to enliven the girl in her mother's lap, and she began to speak softly, sadly. Body language or one-word responses were all she got in return. The girl's eyes fell on Abby and she stared because she had someone's undivided attention. "Ukrainian?" Abby asked.

The girl nodded—it seemed all of them nodded, ever so slightly. Abby wondered how the man escaped with the draft and all, and then she remembered he clearly spoke Polish to their driver, so it wasn't likely that he was an immediate family member. Maybe just a Polish friend of the family. Or another driver making a buck—and expecting to make a few more from her. She thought about her wallet. Maybe she had a twenty left. "Does anyone speak English?" Abby finally asked, trying to sound polite.

"I learn some English in school," the boy squeezed in next to her said softly.

Abby looked down at him and smiled, "That's wonderful. I've been so grateful to meet children who can speak English." The boy smiled wanly, not even looking at her. She wasn't even sure he fully comprehended her compliment, but she pushed on. "Are you escaping the war?"

The boy nodded. "We left Papa. We can't stay."

"What city are you from?"

"Kharkiv. We take train."

"Is that your Grandma?" Abby asked.

The boy shook his head. "We meet her

on train. She know this man driving us."

"That was lucky, meeting her then," Abby smiled at him. The boy nodded solemnly. "Do you know where you're going in Warsaw?" He shook his head and shrugged. Abby decided she had questioned the poor child enough. "You speak good English," she added. The boy nodded again with the same somber expression.

After another hour or so, the woman spoke to the boy and he turned to Abby. "Are you from U.S.A.?"

"Yes I am. This is my granddaughter. She was born in Ukraine and we are taking her home."

The boy looked confused, but told his mother what Abby had said. His mother spoke to him again and he then asked, "Who is we?"

"My son. He stayed with the driver of our car. I will meet him in Warsaw." The boy nodded and told his mother. She also nodded and then they were all quiet again.

The driver pulled into a petrol station and everyone piled out to use the rest rooms. Abby pointed to her bag and the older woman shook her head no, pointing to Jillian, then herself and making a rocking motion. They looked at each other, woman to woman, and Abby gave in, handing Jillian over and making a dash for the toilets. When she returned she found the woman buttoning up the onesies and a dirty diaper on the floor of the car. Abby resisted the urge to check if everything was done right by holding her hands over her heart. The older woman smiled and nodded, picking up the soiled diaper. Abby took it from her and went off to find a garbage can. The others were trudging back to the car when Abby had the idea of doing something nice for them all. She held up a finger and dashed back into the little cashier's office, grabbed six chocolate bars and paid for them with her card. The children, of course, were especially happy with this, but she noticed the man devoured his too, between sips from a thermos. Then he steered the car back onto the highway.

They drove silently and as Abby looked around, she noticed the family and the older woman had all fallen asleep. It was then that Abby realized how exhausted and hungry she was. She looked down at Jillian, amazed at how relatively quiet and calm she had been through this whole ordeal. But then her amazement turned to worry. How could an infant be this placid unless something was wrong with her? She carefully touched Jillian's forehead, hoping her cold hand wouldn't awaken her. She felt okay. And how could something not be wrong with her being in the cold and never changing position in Abby's arms? And then she realized that her arms were sore from holding Jillian in the same position for so long. Her anxiety and fear were now joined by pain and discomfort. Abby took a deep breath and forced herself back against the seat. She exhaled and took in another deep breath, making herself repeat the pattern. Her body relaxed and did not notice when her grip on Jillian loosened. Packed as they were in the back seat, there was no place for her to fall. And she too fell asleep.

They all woke up to honking cars and the continual stop and start of the car. When Abby opened her eyes, she saw tall buildings and hordes of people on sidewalks. They must be in Warsaw. She smiled at the boy, his mother, and his sister. Only the mother smiled back automatically. The driver pulled up in front of a building and said, "U.S.A. Embassy."

Abby inhaled deeply and exhaled with a contented sigh. They had made it. The old lady gave her back her purse and Abby rummaged through it for the twenty-dollar bill she remembered. She found it and handed it to the driver who looked at it and then slipped in into his pocket. "Thank you all," Abby said, giving a silly little wave. "Good luck." The older woman nodded and waved back while the family just looked back soberly. Abby spun around, eager to no longer have to face their sadness. She walked quickly to a revolving door and pushed her way in. "Well . . . we made it, Jillian."

24

THE EMBASSY LOBBY WAS TEEMING WITH PEOPLE. Abby couldn't believe there could be this many Americans trying to get home. The line leading to the receptionist was long and improvised along the walls so people could lean or even sit on the floor and rest. Abby sighed. At least she and Jillian were inside and warm, and in a place where they spoke English. As Abby searched for the end of the line, she noticed a table with water bottles, a coffee urn, and boxes of donuts. She made a beeline for it, took a bottle of water and three plain donuts and stuffed them in her purse. She was suddenly starving and would have eaten a whole prime rib if it had been sitting on the table!

Her arms were aching from carrying Jillian and how she longed for that car seat or a stroller. She wasn't even sure how she'd get the water and doughnuts in her mouth while holding Jillian. She found the end of the line and stood behind a young man about twenty or so. He smiled at her. "Hi," he said, looking at the baby in her arms. "How old?"

"Three weeks," Abby replied, letting a sigh escape her lips.

She put Jillian on her other hip, next to her purse that was hanging off that shoulder, and tried to take out one of the donuts. She had the baby in one arm and the donut in her other hand, and then realized that she had no hand to take down her mask so she could eat. "Can I help you?" the man asked.

"Could you hold the baby while I eat and drink?"

"Sure." The man awkwardly took Jillian out of Abby's arms and she quickly ate one doughnut and then another and then the last. She drank the whole bottle of water in several gulps as the man watched, wide-eyed. "I guess you haven't eaten in awhile," he said, trying not to laugh.

"It's become my nasty habit to eat that way after all this chaos," Abby panted, "but I'll probably regret chugging that water without knowing where the restroom is."

"I'll help you out when the time comes," he said, giving Jillian a bounce for emphasis. "I, uh, presume you came from Ukraine?"

"Yes. What a nightmare. You?"

He nodded. "I was an exchange student there, halfway through my year abroad."

"What partner school did you come from?"

"University of Michigan." He then cocked his head. "You speak like you know how that works."

"I was a teacher back in California," Abby explained. "That's my granddaughter you're holding. She was born in Ukraine by surrogacy." She was on a roll now, once again able to hold a conversation in English and complete sentences.

"You came to get her alone?!" the young man asked incredulously.

"No," chuckled Abby. "My daughter-in-law got Covid—oh," she paused to pull up her mask back over her nose and mouth, "so I came with my son to pick up Jillian."

"And your son is . . .?" he asked, his eyes wandering around the crowd.

"On the road somewhere with the driver who was bringing us here. We got a flat and I got a ride here by . . . well, I needn't go into that. He's supposed to meet me—oh shoot!"

"What's wrong?"

"I need to charge my phone and he has the charger in his backpack."

"Is it an iPhone?"

"Yes."

The man handed Jillian back to Abby and took a charger out of his own backpack. "See if this fits."

Abby gave the baby back to the man and put it in her phone. "It does. But where's an outlet?"

The man scowled and shook his head. "Never mind. I forgot that I lost the voltage adaptor for the charger."

"Oh well," Abby sighed. "Maybe they can help me with it once I get to the front of the line." She reached out her arms to take Jillian.

"I can hold her for a while," he said. "Give your arms a break."

Abby's shoulders fell, relieved of their anticipated burden. "Thank you. You're a godsend." She started shaking out her arms and moved about a foot closer to the reception desk. "My name's Abby."

"Victor."

"Are you Ukrainian?"

"Born in America, but my parents were Ukrainian immigrants."

"Oh wow. So that's why you're here as an exchange student. Your parents must be very happy that you're studying there."

"Maybe," he half smiled. "They died when I was very young."

"Oh, sorry. Did you see relatives while you were there?"

"Well, I was starting to search for them while I was there. I've had no connection with them. I was put into foster care when I was four and a half."

Abby exhaled and shook her head. "Quite a story you have."

The man shrugged. "I was lucky. I had a good foster family and wonderful teachers who helped me. I bet you were a wonderful teacher, too."

It was Abby's turn to shrug. "Well . . ." She couldn't believe she was actually blushing. "So you're from Michigan?"

"No. I went there because it was one of the very few schools where I could minor in Ukrainian studies while majoring in political science. I'm actually from New York City."

"Me too!" Abby exclaimed. "What borough?"

"Brooklyn."

"I grew up in Manhattan." Abby laughed. "I'd say small world, but New York City is so big that it's hard not to run into someone from there."

They chatted comfortably for a while until Jillian started to cry. "Is she hungry?" Victor asked.

"Oh I'm sure. I just hope I have more formula." Abby looked through her bag, but didn't find another bottle. "Damn. No more. Well, we're not too far from the front of the line. I just hope they don't close before we get there. Is your phone charged?" she asked.

"Sorta. Do you want to call someone?"

"I just want to text my son Eric that we are here. His phone is also out of juice, but at least he'll know we got here when he eventually gets it charged." They did the baby exchange again so Victor could take out his phone and then exchanged again.

"How did you do this all by yourself?" Victor chuckled. "I mean, how did you have enough hands?"

"It's amazing what you do when you have no choice." Abby texted Eric and once again they did the baby exchange. She then studied the crowd. "I guess all these people are trying to get back to America."

"I don't know. Maybe they just want to stay here in Poland until the war is over."

Abby looked at him quizzically. "Do you want to stay here in Poland or go back to Michigan?"

"I want to go back to Kyiv. I'd just as soon stay there if I knew the war would be over soon."

"I guess I hadn't even thought of that. Do you really think the war will be over soon?"

He shrugged. "I'm hoping the embassy can give me some guidance."

They continued to chat as the line inched forward and there were just a few people from the front when a man spoke loudly from the front. "We are closing for the night, but there are buses out front that can take you to a shelter. You can return in the morning at nine."

"Will we lose our place in line?" Victor called out.

"I'm sorry. We're doing the best we can," the man replied.

"Oh no!" Abby's voice cracked. She was ready to cry. "I don't believe this!"

"Don't worry," Victor replied. "It'll be alright. I'll get up early and get in line, and when you arrive I'll have your place saved for you."

"You might have a fight on your hands." He put up his dukes and made a mean face. "Well, alright," Abby laughed. "I'm so glad I met you."

"Me too," he smiled.

The bus took them to a beautiful church and they were ushered inside. There were piles of blankets and pillows, both encased in plastic, with the familiar Red Cross symbol on it. Abby laughed aloud in spite of herself and Victor gave her a dark look. "Sorry. It's not funny, but I never imagined myself in a situation like this. I guess I'm just nervous."

The look on Victor's face didn't totally fade. "You've always had money?"

"Well . . . I've always been comfortable. A house. Food and necessities. I guess you had hard times in foster care?"

"Not really But lean times, yes. I remember stuff like this. Government surplus wrapped in plastic like this. Food pantries."

"Were you in several different homes?"

"Just two. The first one didn't work out well, but I had to stay for several years until they found me one where I stayed until I was eighteen. You know you get kicked out of the system when you turn eighteen."

"Yeah. I knew that. Then you went to college at eighteen?"

Victor nodded. "That's when my teacher helped me so much."

"She counseled you in applying for college?"

"Oh no. She was a teacher I had in elementary school, not high school. She just always kept in touch with me and encouraged me. She got me through tough times, that's all."

Abby smiled, remembering some of the students she'd had that had written her later to thank her. "Well, I guess we take a blanket and pillow and find a pew to sleep on."

"And there's food over there on that big table," Victor pointed.

Abby looked over and saw sandwiches and drinks, granola bars and bags of chips. "Let's find a place to sleep and then take turns going to the food table." Abby held Jillian while Victor carried the plastic covered blankets and pillows and set them down on adjacent pews.

"How are you going to sleep with Jillian?" he asked. "We could take turns."

"Oh, I couldn't ask you to do that."

Victor's silence was enough said. Abby looked around and finally caught the eye of a volunteer wearing a Red Cross tee shirt. The woman zigzagged amidst the pews and finally arrived within speaking distance. "Do you need formula and diapers?" She looked around at their belongings. "And a stroller for the baby to sleep in?"

The very idea of being set free from holding Jillian twenty four/seven let loose a flood of emotions. Abby burst into tears. "Yes! Oh, I'm so sorry—it's just that I'm so tired."

The woman reached out and patted her shoulder. "I'll get them all just as soon as I can."

Victor came close and put his arm around her. "I'm sorry," she sobbed.

"Shhh," Victor murmured, pulling her to his chest. His phone rang and he took it from his pocket. "I think this is your son," he said, handing it to her and stepping back.

"Yes!" she cried, looking at the screen. She took a deep breath and answered. "Eric! Where are you?"

"Back at the car."

"Oh."

"We're getting ready to leave. We had to get the tire to a garage by ourselves to get air in it. And then get a ride back to the car. At least I could charge my phone while our driver was out trying to get a ride back. Are you at the embassy?"

"No. They closed for the night before I could get to the front of the line. They bussed us to a church and the Red Cross provided blankets and pillows, and food, and stuff for Jillian. They even had a stroller!"

"Yeah, there were even a couple of strollers outside the garage for anyone to take."

"Oh wow! Wonderful people the Poles!"

"So whose phone is this?"

"My new friend Victor." She looked at him and smiled. "He's a student at the University of Michigan who was in Ukraine for a year abroad. He's been a lifesaver!"

"I won't tell Brian," Eric chuckled.

"Silly!"

"Well, I hope to meet him tomorrow. And don't forget to charge your phone."

"Yes. I'm sure the Red Cross has something here. You can always call this number." She then glanced at the battery icon. "Oh, Victor's phone is very low, too."

"I'll see you at the embassy tomorrow morning."

"Yes! Love you, dear son."

"Love you too, Mom."

She handed the phone back to Victor. "You stay here and wait for the baby stuff," he said. "I'll get us some food."

Abby started to say she was a vegetarian and there were other things she didn't eat, and then realized how absurd that was in the circumstances. She'd eat whatever he brought back. The lady returned pushing a stroller that had three premade bottles of formula and three diapers on the seat. "That ought to get you through the night," the woman said. "We should have more supplies in the morning."

"Oh perfect," Abby murmured. "Thank you."

The woman nodded and asked, "Do you need anything else?"

"Is there someplace to charge our phones?"

"Oh yes, over there" The woman pointed to a corner of the large room. "There are chargers there for iPhones and I'm not sure what other ones."

"Oh, ours are iPhones. Thanks again."

Victor returned with food and water just as Abby finished changing Jillian's diaper. "We can charge our phones over there," Abby reported, "under that gorgeous stained glass window with the birds and trees."

"Okay. I'll take some food with me and keep an eye on them."

"Thank you," she replied, taking her dead phone out of her purse and handing it over. "I'm so glad you're not a stranger anymore." Victor smiled and went off. Abby got Jillian settled in with a bottle while munching on a granola bar.

"Finally it feels like we are on the home stretch," she murmured as Jillian watched her above the bottle. After Jillian finished, Abby put her in the stroller and dropped the back flat. "Probably this is the most comfortable you've been for days too." Then she looked at the hard pew she'd be sleeping on and chuckled. "Hard to believe that this will be the most comfortable I've been for days!"

Abby ate the sandwich, taking the meat out and leaving the cheese, and then the bag of chips. She wanted to use a restroom, but realized she either had to take Jillian with her or wait for Victor to come back. Her phone had been so dead, though, that it would probably take hours to charge it up. She made up two pews to look like beds so no one would take them and then pushed the stroller to the charging area. Victor was sitting on the floor, his head leaning against the wall with his eyes closed. She then went to the food table and they directed her to the rest rooms. When she arrived back at her pew, she lay down with the stroller by her head. She started to worry about falling asleep. She had grown so used to sleeping with Jillian in her arms—what if someone stole her while she slept? She turned her head and looked at her granddaughter sleeping so close she could hear her breathing. Stop worrying. This is a refuge. We're safe. She closed her eyes and quickly fell asleep.

25

SOMETHING WOKE ABBY OUT OF A DEEP SLEEP. Her eyes snapped open and she looked over at Jillian. In the semi darkness she could see Jillian staring back at her, demanding attention. "Oh, you—," she chuckled, struggling to a sitting position. "Ow!" Abby sighed and rubbed her back, then picked up Jillian out of the stroller. She stood there, looking around the church glowing in a faint colored light from the stained glass window. Most everyone still seemed asleep. Good. She'd be the first on the bus. The pew next to her was empty—obviously Victor had left early, as he planned. Suddenly thinking of her phone, she gave a start, then relaxed. Surely he left it somewhere. Tucked into her purse, most likely—and there it was. She opened it and smiled at the fully charged symbol.

Abby put Jillian back into the stroller along with her purse and pushed her way to the food table, hoping to find a volunteer nearby. No one seemed to be around, but then she sensed something coming up behind her. She turned to see an old woman rolling up to her in a wheelchair. Abby smiled self-consciously and the old woman flashed a toothless smile back at her. Now beside her, the woman reached out and touched her arm. "Dytyna," she whispered, her hand shaking.

"Sorry. I don't speak Polish," Abby replied. "I'm American."

"Dytyna, Ukraine," the woman pleaded softly.

"Oh. You're Ukrainian?" The old woman nodded. "I thought there were only Americans here," Abby said. The old woman just stared, a desperate look in her eyes. Abby alternately frowned and smiled at the awkward situation, slowly realizing that this woman probably needed to use the restroom. And Abby did too, come to think of it, but she'd rather not do bathroom duties for a stranger. A man suddenly appeared, carrying a tower of pink pastry boxes. "Oh!" Abby piped up. "When does the bus leave for the embassy?"

"I'm not sure," he replied. "Maybe in an hour or so."

"How far is it to walk?"

"Several kilometers."

Abby tried to wrap that around her head. It was probably not that far, mile-wise. But it would be icy outside, so she'd have to walk slowly. She probably wouldn't get there much sooner than the bus. She shivered at the thought of being out in the cold. She'd wait. Again the old woman touched her arm. Without a glance in that direction, Abby asked, "Does anyone here speak Ukrainian?"

"You're speaking English."

"Not for me," Abby replied, tilting her head. "Her."

"Oh." It was obvious he was trying to ignore the old woman, too. He began speaking to her and she spoke back rapidly. "She's hoping you'll help her in the restroom."

"Well, of course," Abby faltered, "but how can I push a stroller and a wheelchair?"

"She followed you under her own power, didn't she?" the man replied, trying to hide a smile.

"Why is she here?" Abby asked bluntly.

"We don't turn anyone away." He then spoke to the woman and she replied. "She says she has a daughter in America, so she's hoping the embassy can help her."

"I see." Abby took a deep breath and put on a smile. She turned to the old woman and motioned her to follow. She turned back to the man. "What is dytyna?"

"Dytyna means baby."

"Ah," Abby now understood what the old woman was saying.

In the restroom the woman was able to point and mimic what she needed help with. Abby ignored Jillian's crying so she could get the woman's and her own restroom duties done with as quickly as possible. They finally left the restroom and Abby made a beeline for the door so that she would be ready as soon as the bus arrived. The old woman followed right behind her. Abby tried to bury her annoyance. The last thing she needed was yet another person depending on her. Minutes passed and her thoughts softened over the idea of an old woman alone in a wheelchair fleeing her homeland. Abby hiked Jillian up onto her hip again, duly aware of her relative mobility.

The bus finally came and several people pitched in to help with the stroller and the wheelchair. A couple of men fairly launched the old woman onto the bus with a shove on her ample rear end. The woman started laughing, and that started everyone else laughing. None of this phased Jillian, as she had been cranky since being ignored in the restroom. Once the woman plopped herself into the nearest seat, she leaned over and tried to entertain Jillian with silly faces. Jillian was having none of it, though. Despite the racket, Abby was moved by the woman's sense of humor and she felt resigned to the unhappy situation.

They arrived at the embassy and there was already a long line out front. They got out of the bus, again with help from other passengers, and Abby rushed ahead to the front of the line, looking frantically for Victor. She couldn't see him but heard a voice calling, "Abby! Over here!" She looked around and finally saw him waving at her. He wasn't at the front of the line, but only about ten people back. She started for him, but then looked back at the old woman forlornly watching her. Abby waved for the woman to follow her.

"Victor!" Abby said as she rushed up and impulsively hugged him. "This lady is Ukrainian and doesn't speak English. Someone got it out of her that she fled and is trying to get to America to be with her daughter." Abby then shrugged. "She's kind of hooked herself onto me."

"The more the merrier," Victor smiled.

"Well, the rest of the line might not think so."

"The guy behind me knows your story and I told him to pass it along. No one better complain about an old lady in a wheelchair being added to the mix." He grinned and playfully showed a fist, then bent down to speak to the woman.

The woman spoke fast and furious and Victor tried to answer her. "Do you understand her?" Abby asked.

"Mostly. I just can't answer quickly. I still have to think about how to say it."

"That's how I am with French. I took it in school for many years, from the first grade on. I can read it and understand it, but can't speak it. Are the doors open yet?"

"Soon, I think."

"I should see if my son Eric's here yet." Abby looked up and down the line that was getting longer by the minute.

"Why don't you take a walk and see. I'll take care of Jillian and um . . ." He turned to the old woman and spoke to her. "Her name is Oksana."

Abby nodded and left Victor, Jillian and Oksana to walk up and down the line. She came back and said, "He's not here yet. Maybe I'll text him so he knows where we are." She did that and waited for a reply, but none came. "Well, hopefully he'll be here before my turn comes."

Victor sighed "I hope so too. I—" he paused, "I've decided to go back to Ukraine."

"What? Why?"

"To fight."

Abby's mouth dropped. "You would put yourself in that kind of danger when you don't have to? You're American."

"I know. But I want to."

"Oh Victor. Are you sure?"

"Yes. I'm sure. But I won't leave you until you find your son."

Abby sighed and looked over at the old woman and was reminded of what this war was about. She and Jillian and Eric would be home, safe and sound, soon enough. Oksana and Victor were Ukrainians. This was about them. Abby was just caught in the middle. The line finally started to inch forward. "I guess they finally opened," she said. "Will the university let you take off the time to fight?"

Victor shrugged. "I'm not sure I care. I feel like this is much more important."

"In some ways, I guess. But what you're studying is also important to help gain freedom and democracy for Ukraine."

"That makes no impression on Putin," Victor retorted. "War does. And Ukraine has to win this."

Abby's phone dinged and she dug it out of her purse, hoping it was Eric. It wasn't. It was Brian asking where she was and what she was doing and pleading with her to call or at least text him. "It's my husband in the states." She sighed. "I'll just text him that I'm in line at the embassy and will call when I have a definitive plan."

"He must be very worried."

Abby nodded and added to her text for him to text Heather, in case Eric hadn't. She kept straining her neck to look all around the crowd for her son. "I wonder where Eric is. He called last night and it should have been only a few hours to get here."

"Maybe he's inside already, waiting for you. We're getting closer. Hang in there." Victor smiled and patted her shoulder.

"Ask Oksana how she's doing."

Victor spoke to Oksana who answered with a shrug. "She's cold and hungry and scared," he replied to Abby.

"Does her daughter know that she's at the embassy?"

Victor and Oksana exchanged some words. "No. She hasn't been able to get a hold of her."

"Tell her she can try again with my phone," Abby said, handing her phone to Victor.

More Ukrainian conversation and Victor handed the phone back to Abby. "She wants to wait until the embassy people tell her what to do."

"I can't believe she's come all this way alone in a wheelchair."

"She told me earlier that her son had gotten her to the border and on a bus that took her to Warsaw, so she's only been alone overnight. She probably got caught up in a similar situation as we did."

Finally they got to the door and Abby pushed the stroller inside while Victor pushed Oksana's wheelchair. "We made it!" Abby hugged Victor. She looked around the room, hoping to find Eric leaning against a wall waiting for her. She didn't see him, but her phone rang and it was Eric. "Are you at the embassy?" Abby asked breathlessly.

"I'm outside. Are you in line?"

"I'm inside almost to the front."

"Okay. Now we're going to have to try to explain to everyone in front of me that I get to go ahead of them!"

"Tell them about the grandma with the baby up ahead. Victor has been sending that story down the line. Maybe it's gone that far back." Abby ended the call and turned to Victor. "He's outside, trying to push his way in."

"Is he the kind of guy that will do that?" Victor laughed.

"Not usually, but let's hope he has it in him at a time like this." Abby paused, deep in thought. "We should let Oksana go first. I really need to wait for Eric because I'm not Jillian's parent."

They finally got to the front of the line. "This is Oksana," Abby told the clerk. "She's a Ukrainian refugee who doesn't speak English and is trying to get to her daughter in America."

"I need to get a translator," the clerk said.

"I can try to explain. I speak it some," Victor interjected.

"That's okay." The clerk got up and went into a back office. She returned with a man who spoke to Oksana.

"Is she related to you?" the man asked Abby and Victor.

"No. She's alone. She was sheltering at the same church we were at."

"I see." He turned to the female clerk. "I'll take her." He started to wheel Oksana away when she started yelling at him. He turned her around to face Abby. Tears streamed down her face and she spoke to the male clerk. "She said to thank you and God bless you."

Abby went over to the wheelchair and hugged Oksana. "Please tell her good luck." The man nodded and wheeled her away.

The female clerk was talking to Victor and then turned to Abby. "You're waiting for your son?"

"He's outside, trying to get in. He has all the paperwork for the baby."

"Then who are you?" the clerk asked Victor.

"I'm an American student who was studying at Taras Shevchenko National University of Kyiv. I have decided to go back to Ukraine and fight. I am just helping them until her son gets here."

The clerk looked at him skeptically. "Okay, but step aside so I can help the next person." She turned to Abby. "You, too. Wait here until your son gets inside."

Abby nodded and turned to Victor. "I'll be fine now."

"Are you sure? I can wait."

"I'm sure." She hugged him. "Take care of yourself. And thank you for everything. Let's see . . . your number will be in Eric's phone. I will text you soon so you have mine. Please stay in contact. I'll be worrying about you."

Victor hugged her back and touched Jillian's cheek. "You're a resilient, sweet baby. You'll go far in life." Victor left and Abby wiped a tear off her cheek. And then Jillian started to wail.

"Oh baby, it won't be that long before we're home." Abby tried to comfort Jillian as she scanned the room and finally saw Eric approaching them.

"Thanks for the siren call, Jillian!" Eric cried, swooping down and unbuckling her from the stroller. He held her high and Abby threw her arms around her son.

26

THE CLERK WATCHED THE LITTLE REUNION OUT OF THE CORNER OF HER EYE. When she finished with the latest person at the counter, she called Abby over. Abby introduced Eric and let him do all the talking. She stepped back, scanning the large lobby filled with people trying to get to America. She wondered if she might meet Oksana again or even end up on the same plane. Since she never did learn where her daughter lived, that didn't seem likely. As she completed her survey of the situation, she became aware of Eric's agitated voice, so she turned back to the counter.

"I'm sorry, sir," the clerk seemed to repeat, "but she needs a doctor's note that she's healthy enough to travel before I can issue a passport."

"How and where are we going to get that note?" Eric demanded. "I know nothing about Warsaw!"

"Perhaps you could go to a clinic or hospital."

"Perhaps I could, if I knew where one was! We can't be the only people in this situation here!"

"I'm sorry, but—"

"For heaven's sake!" Abby snapped. "I just carried this three-week-old baby through a war zone and I think that's quite enough for her short time on this planet! Now go and find someone who can cut through all this red tape!"

The clerk sighed and went into the back office to speak to the man who had taken Oksana. Abby and Eric watched for several minutes as he kept shaking his head. When she returned, she was wearing something between a scowl and sadness. "We need the note. I'm sorry. My supervisor suggested you go to the hospital. I wrote down the address."

"Is it far? Can we walk?" Eric asked.

"I don't know. I'm not from here. I was reassigned from Kyiv."

"So," Abby cut in, "if we go to the hospital and get a note, do we have to wait in this endless line again?"

"All these people are as anxious as you are to get home. I'm sorry."

Abby took a deep breath and glanced over at Eric with an eye roll. She then snatched the paper from the clerk's hand. "And would you happen to have diapers and formula?" she asked too sweetly.

"They were delivered to the church, I believe. You were there last night, right?"

"Yes, and the pews were divine."

"Mom-m," Eric hissed. "Let's get to the damn hospital and get the stupid note so we can get back before the end of the day." She spun the stroller around for effect, banging it one someone's ankle. "Oh! So sorry," Eric apologized as Abby continued on her way. "She's just a bit upset." The victim glared at him, so he beat a hasty retreat. "Mom," Eric said, catching up to her. "If you're not careful we could be barred from here!"

"Don't pretend you're not as furious as I am."

"Mom! Stop! I need to find the address on my phone." Abby stopped and made a sound like a train expelling its air brakes. Eric tapped at his phone for a while. "Okay. Now give me the stroller. I haven't had any quality time with my daughter for days. Let's just move on."

"Walking?"

"It's less than two miles," Eric replied. "We wouldn't save any time looking for a ride, really, especially with this stroller and all the traffic."

"True." Abby hitched up her pants. "I think I've lost ten pounds on this trip."

"I'm starving. I'm looking forward to the cafeteria at the hospital," Eric sighed

"Said no one ever."

"Well, how many people have been through something like this?" Abby said nothing, but wrapped her hand over his as he pushed the stroller through the crowded sidewalks. Eric stopped frequently to consult his phone. "Are you doing okay?" he asked.

"Couldn't be better." They trudged along and finally saw the hospital. The first thing Abby did when they got inside was look for a restroom. "I'll go first and then I can watch Jillian while you go."

"I'm okay. I'll try to get some help." Eric went to a desk that he assumed was admitting. "Do you speak English?"

The nurse at the desk put up a finger and went to get someone else. She came back with another woman. "What do you need?" the second woman asked. Eric proceeded to tell her of their predicament and then asked for a diaper and formula and the doctor's note. "Come," she motioned him to follow.

"I need to wait for my mother. She's in the restroom." The woman nodded and they stood there for a moment in silence until Abby approached.

"You buy diapers and formula at pharmacy," the woman explained. Eric nodded. "You go to Emergency to see doctor."

"Wouldn't the emergency department have formula and diapers?" Abby cut in.

"Diapers. No formula. I take you to emergency." The woman pushed her way through a door, Abby and Eric struggling to keep up with her. They got to the emergency department and the woman spoke to the nurse sitting at the counter, then came back to them. "She say sit here and she find English-speaking doctor."

"Thank you," Eric said as the woman walked away. He turned to Abby. "I'll use the restroom and then look for where to get formula and food for us."

"What if they call us in while you're gone?"

He shrugged. "Text me and I'll come right away. It's not like I'll be gone that long."

Abby nodded, a little frightened of being left alone again in a foreign environment. Jillian became fussy, so she took her out of the stroller and tried to entertain her, but to no avail. At least it kept her mind off the situation, though. When Eric returned, Jillian was outright crying. "This girl needs a bottle and a diaper," Abby announced. Eric handed over both, plus a granola bar and a bag of chips. "I am so sick of chips," Abby sighed.

"That was all I could readily recognize there. I was in a hurry, you know. Maybe there's a cafeteria—"

"I don't want to waste time eating in a cafeteria," Abby interrupted. "I want to get back to the embassy before they close."

Jillian quieted down as soon as they got on a clean diaper and a bottle in her mouth. She was fast asleep in the stroller when they were called into a room. Eric explained the situation to the doctor as briefly as he could, adding that they would appreciate it if he could hurry through the exam so they could get back to the embassy. The doctor nodded, saying very little as he examined her. "They checked her at the hospital in Kyiv where she was born. Here's their report," Eric said, handing the doctor a piece of paper.

"She's healthy. I'll get the note written." He left the room.

"Oh thank goodness!" Abby exclaimed. "Something is finally going our way."

"Are you surprised that she's healthy?"

"No. I was just afraid they were going to have to do a bunch of tests or something and it would take much longer."

"I think we have plenty of time to get back to the embassy."

"As long as the doctor doesn't keep us waiting for that note," Abby retorted.

A nurse arrived shortly with an envelope and handed it to Eric. "Thank you." He opened the envelope and saw that it was written in Polish. "I hope they don't have to get this translated before giving us Jillian's passport."

They followed the nurse out of the room, down the hall, and through the doors into the waiting area. "Do you remember how to get back to the embassy?" Abby asked.

Eric looked at her quizzically. "Don't you?"

"That's one of the reasons I like having you around," she grinned at him. "I don't have to remember how to get anywhere." Almost an hour later they arrived at the embassy and, of course, there was a long line. "What time is it?"

Eric looked at his phone. "A little after one."

"I hope they don't close for a late lunch," Abby muttered.

"I doubt they would do that at a time like this."

The line moved slowly, when it moved at all. It was cold and starting to snow and Jillian started to get antsy. "I'm going to take her inside," Abby said. "I won't push to the front of the line, but I'll tell people that I'm just taking the baby inside. You stay in line." Abby took the stroller and people happily moved out of her way as she explained what she was doing. When she got to the door the woman standing there said, "You get in front of me with that baby."

"Are you sure?"

"Yes."

"Well, I'm not," the man behind her snarled.

"Well, aren't you the doting grandpa!" the woman shot back.

"I'm not a grandpa!"

"That's because no woman would ever lay with you. Now shut your trap." Abby almost laughed except for the vicious glare he threw at her.

"Lay off, old man," said another man behind him. "I saw her here earlier with a younger man."

"My son," Abby piped up. "Her daddy," she added, rocking the stroller for emphasis.

With a huff the old man turned away to look at nothing in particular, so Abby motioned to Eric. "This lovely woman is letting us go ahead of her," she said as he approached.

"Thanks so much," Eric smiled as together they pushed the stroller inside the building. Again they inched along. "I just hope we don't have to wait long for her passport," he murmured to Abby.

"It's crazy how they demand a passport for a newborn of American citizens," scoffed Abby.

"At least we didn't have to adopt our own child, like some countries require," Eric sighed. "And there are ugly reasons why a passport is required, like baby trafficking. Without a passport, Jillian is as easy a target as any undocumented baby."

"Oh," Abby shivered. "I didn't think of that."

Over an hour passed by the time they made it back to the counter. Eric slapped the envelope onto the counter. "We have the note from a doctor."

The woman opened the envelope and glanced over the note. "Okay. But it will still take some time to get the papers in order."

"Why?" Abby asked. "We have everything we need."

The woman sighed. "Covid had made things more difficult, and now the war." She looked through the papers again and said, "Where's the picture?"

"Picture?" Abby asked.

"For the passport. You need a picture of the baby."

"Seriously? But she's going to change so much."

"You still need one for the passport."

"Well I have a ton on my phone," Eric said. He opened his photos and showed them to the clerk.

"It needs to be a serious expression with her eyes open."

Eric scrolled through the pictures and found one. "Will this work?"

"Yes. But you have to get it printed."

"I can't just text or email it to you?"

"No."

"He can't just send it to you and then you print it out here?" Abby asked with exasperation.

The clerk shook her head. "Can you direct me somewhere close by where I can print it?" Eric asked.

"No," sighed the clerk. I just came from Kyiv, remember?"

"How long do you think it will take to get the passport after we give you the picture?"

The woman shrugged. "At least a week. Maybe longer."

Eric looked over at his mother with a shocked expression. "We can't stay at that church for a week!" Abby cried.

"I have a list of hotels and hostels," the clerk offered.

"That would be helpful," Eric muttered. He looked over at Abby. "At least prices in Poland are as cheap as Ukraine."

The clerk handed Eric a list. "I would call first and make sure they have rooms."

"You mean there might not be any?!" Abby cried.

"Mom," Eric sighed. "Where do you think all these people are staying?"

"Friends? Family? Churches?" Abby glared at him.

"Give me your phone number and I'll make copies of all your paperwork," offered the clerk. "I'll try to expedite this as best I can. But I still need the picture before I can actually make up the passport."

"Thank you," replied Eric wearily. As the clerk made copies he stood aside and made some phone calls. Abby could tell by his expression that he wasn't getting anywhere. The clerk returned with the paperwork and they escaped further into a corner of the lobby, where Eric continued calling. She tried not to listen. It was too depressing. "Okay, Mom," he finally said, getting her attention. "There's a private room at a hostel about half a mile from here."

"A hostel? Do they have private rooms? I thought they were all like dormitories."

"This one has a private room and it's available, so I reserved it."

"But we share a bathroom, right?"

"Mom, you've been sharing restrooms for like a week, haven't you?"

"Yes . . ." She wished for a bath: a private tub to soak in until next week.

"And it's a bed, not a pew."

"Yes . . ." And at least there was a door to shut out the world.

"Okay, then—let's go."

27

ERIC OPENED THE DOOR TO THEIR ROOM AT THE HOSTEL AND ABBY PEERED IN. It was very narrow, with a chair, a sink, hooks on the wall and bunk beds. Abby snorted and then started laughing hysterically. "So who gets the top bunk?"

"You do!" Eric snapped, pushing past her.

"Seriously. Bunk beds."

"Better than pews."

"I'm not so sure, with you above me," she winked.

"Since that's been decided," Eric muttered, throwing his backpack on the upper bunk. He then unfolded the stroller and placed Jillian in it. "Any more ideas?"

"Eating?"

"There's a communal kitchen downstairs, so I guess we could go shopping." Eric paused and then sighed. "But I'm too tired. We can go shopping and get the picture printed in the morning."

"Well, I want you to rest, but . . ."

"Why don't you find a restaurant and get us something to eat?"

"Uh, okay," she replied hesitantly.

"What's wrong?"

"I don't know. I guess I'm a little uncomfortable walking around by myself."

"Um, Mom. You were flagging down motorists just the other night."

"I know, but it's so hard when you don't speak the language."

"Okay, you're obviously tired, too. Do you want me to get us food?"

"No," she replied, making herself sound more resolute than she felt. "I want you to sleep. What about Jillian?"

"Just leave her."

"But she might wake you up."

"Mom. I'll have years of not sleeping ahead of me with Jillian, so I might as well get used to it. Besides, unlike you, I can fall asleep again easily."

"Okay. Any ideas where restaurants are?"

Eric sighed. "You don't remember all the places we passed walking over here?"

"Okay. Okay. I guess you don't care what I get?"

"No, Mom. I don't care at all."

"Do we have enough formula for the next couple of feedings?"

"Yes. I still have several bottles."
"And diapers?"

"Yes. Enough until tomorrow."

"Okay. I guess I can't procrastinate any longer." Abby smiled, picked up her purse and left.

Abby returned with a salad for herself, kielbasa for Eric, and pierogies for them both. She even bought some Babka, a kind of marble cake. They ate heartily, gave Jillian a sponge bath and fed her, and then called their respective spouses to update them. Abby also called Paige, and Eric called his work to explain why he had been incognito and not done any work at all for the last few days. By the time all this was finished, they fell into their respective bunks and slept hard. Eventually they were awakened by Jillian's crying. "I'll take her," Eric said, tumbling down from above.

Abby opened her eyes a bit later. "What time is it?"

Eric looked at his phone. "Eight-thirty."

"I can't wait to take a shower. How does one do that here?"

"In the bathroom?"

"I mean, is there a schedule or something?"

"Just go and use the shower. I'll go after you. Don't overthink this, Mom."

Abby left for her shower and Eric got Jillian up and had her diapered and fed by the time Abby returned. "Well, that was very interesting . . . but fun. People are nice and friendly." She laughed. "They all made room for the old lady."

"Good to hear. It's my turn now. And then we'll hit the grocery store."

"Do you really think we're going to be here for more than a week?" Abby asked.

"I don't know. But I've been thinking about just trying to get on a plane without Jillian's passport."

Abby's eyes widened. "Do you think it would work?"

Eric shrugged. "The worst thing that could happen would be they don't let us on the plane and then we'd be back exactly where we are now."

"That's true. Let's try. Do you think Uber is available here?"

"Of course."

"I mean because of the war."

- - -

"The war isn't here."

"It kind of is with all the refugees."

"Well, that's what I'm hoping will get us on a plane," Eric replied. "They'll want to get rid of us."

"So should we still go grocery shopping?"

"Yes. Just buy stuff we can take with us. We might be in the airport awhile."

"What about this room? What if we don't get on the plane and the room gets rented."

"We could pay for tonight and then not use it, I guess."

"Good idea."

They went shopping and bought nuts, fruit, and bread — stuff that didn't have to be refrigerated — as well as diapers and formula. They found a place to get Jillian's picture printed and although it was a challenge because they couldn't speak Polish, they finally got it done. They also stopped at a restaurant and bought a hearty lunch to bring back to their room. Eric had some kind of Polish goulash called bigos overflowing with pork while Abby bought some vegetarian stuffed cabbage called golabki. "Should we stop at the embassy before we go to the airport and drop off the picture?"

"I think that's a good idea," Eric answered. "We probably have to get Covid tested before we go. I wonder if they come to us or there's somewhere we can go."

"Maybe someone here knows."

"I'll go downstairs and see if anyone's there and ask." Eric left and returned several minutes later. "They said there are clinics and pharmacies that do the tests, but you can also get one at the airport."

"Then let's do that," Abby replied.

They packed up their things and Eric tapped the Uber app. "It says the car will be here in twenty minutes."

"Oh gosh, I hope this works. I really don't want to hang around here for another week."

They went downstairs and waited several minutes until the car got there. They stopped at the embassy and Eric pushed his way to the front, telling everyone in line that he was just dropping something off. That didn't go over well, but he managed to do it and they got to the airport less than half an hour later. The traffic was not bad at all, something they had not been used to these last few days. They piled out of the car at a testing site at the airport, got tested, and waited for results. Meanwhile, Eric looked for flights to San Francisco and found them all full. "I guess we'll have to try standby."

"Oh, let's not," sighed Abby. "The airport isn't far from the hostel and we're paid up for the night. Are there seats on a plane tomorrow?"

"I'll look." As Eric looked at his phone, he got a text saying the tests were negative.

"I wonder how long these tests are good for," Abby said.

"I'm sure they'll still be good tomorrow, at least."

"So what do you want to do?"

Eric exhaled. "Since we're already here, let's see what they say at the ticket counter."

They walked inside the terminal and were greeted by an almost impenetrable crowd of people.

"This is nuts!" Abby yelled above the din. "Even if we had tickets!"

"Well, we're here now so we might as well try to get on a flight."

"Okay." Abby groaned. They got on what looked like a line leading to the ticket counter, but it was hard to tell where the line began and ended. People seemed to break in and out of line and after an hour it was obvious why; the line wasn't going anywhere. "Eric, why don't you just go to the counter and ask if there are any flights to the U.S. It seems crazy to be standing on this line for no reason if nothing comes of it. The lack of Jillian's passport is one thing, but if there aren't even any seats left anyway . . ."

"I guess." Eric pushed to the counter. "Are there any seats left to the U.S.?" he shouted.

"No sir," a clerk shouted back, not even looking in his direction. "Not today."

Eric went back to Abby. "Let's just go and see what I can do online about getting tickets."

They hustled out the door and briefly pulled down their masks and took a deep breath of fresh air. Nearby there was a line of cars under an Uber sign and Eric told the driver the name of the hostel. Before they knew it, they were back in their old room. Eric immediately went online looking for plane tickets. "Any luck?" Abby asked, looking up at his mattress sagging over her head.

"It's only getting worse. There are no tickets for several days."

"What about getting tickets out of Warsaw to some European country further west first?"

"I don't know," Eric sighed. "I'm beginning to feel like we should just stay until we get the passport and then let the embassy find us plane seats."

Abby didn't know how to answer. She knew Eric was probably right, but she hated the idea of staying for another week or more. But at least they had a somewhat comfortable place to sleep and there was food, a bathroom, heat . . . "Maybe you're right," she finally replied.

They still weren't interested in cooking although there was a communal kitchen downstairs, so they ended up with pizza and salad. After they ate Abby said, "Did you pay for a week?"

"Dang. I forgot. I'd better go do that." He grabbed his wallet and rushed out the door. When he returned he had a frown on his face. "Bad news. It is rented starting tomorrow. All they have is a couple of beds in a room with two other people."

"Well, that won't work with a baby and all. Now what?"

"Search for another room, of course."

"If we're going to be here for at least another week, we need to find someplace comfortable."

"Since you know what you want, why don't you look for it?"

Abby frowned. "Where are we?"

Eric rolled his eyes. "Warsaw, Mom. Open a map and it'll show you with a blue dot exactly where you are. Better yet, type in 'American Embassy Warsaw' and it'll show what's nearby. Or do the same with a hotel app."

"Wouldn't a map be better?" Abby asked, opening her computer. "It would show me everything nearby, not just who's on the app."

"Probably, but you're likely to run into a language barrier."

"Not if I use their website."

Eric didn't think that was necessarily so, but wanted to encourage her and be done with it. "See, you know what you're doing." He went over and took Jillian out of the stroller and started talking to her, making up simple little games. Abby was quiet for quite some time.

"Some of these sites aren't in English," Abby finally said.

"Because you're in Poland," Eric replied, not missing a beat with Jillian. "Look in the corners of the page and see if there's an English icon."

Abby continued typing and muttering to herself. "Score!" she finally announced. "Two beds and a private bath two kilometers from the embassy for fifty bucks a night!"

"Congratulations."

Abby tilted the screen. "It looks like it's near a highway interchange."

"Said the woman who never sleeps anyway."

"I was thinking about Jillian."

"I haven't noticed anything stopping her from sleeping except her own stomach and diaper."

"Okay, then," Abby replied, typing again. "It looks really nice on the website. And there are cafes and restaurants all around it. I'm booking it for a week, just to be sure."

"Great."

"I can't wait for our own bathroom," Abby sighed, shutting her computer. "I guess I'll get ready for bed. Do you want me to feed Jillian or anything first?"

"I'll do it," Eric replied, rummaging through his backpack. "I guess I'll go heat a bottle in the kitchen since I can."

He was gone for much longer than necessary. "There you are!" Abby exclaimed as he finally entered the room. "I was starting to worry."

"There were some Americans in the kitchen. We were debating what to do next."

"Oh!" Abby cried. "Any new ideas?"

"Not really," Eric sighed. "They're going to the airport in the morning and just stay there until they can get on a flight. They're not even attempting to go to the U.S. directly. They're trying to get on a flight to France or England."

Abby slumped down in the chair. "We may have to do that, too, then."

"Well let's not get ahead of ourselves. Maybe we can try to enjoy a week in Warsaw."

Abby glanced up at him incredulously. "You're kidding, right?"

28

THE NEXT MORNING THEY DECIDED TO SKIP THE SHOWER AT THE HOSTEL AND MOVE INTO THE HOTEL AS SOON AS POSSIBLE. Upon arriving they found out that their room wouldn't be ready for several hours, so they left the hotel and wandered around. Besides museums and churches there were countless cafes and bars, not to mention the ubiquitous Pizza Hut and Hard Rock Café found in most any European city. They managed to laugh at the irony of empty American culture being so close at hand, but home being so inaccessible. Abby shook her head at the blast of music and cigarette smoke coming out of the Hard Rock. "Just like old times," she chuckled.

We could go to a museum," Eric offered, although he would have preferred to just wander about and stare at people. Or take a nap.

"I think we need new KN-95's for that," Abby replied, digging onto her purse. "Museums are usually so airless. Let's see—I have two left."

"Maybe we should save them for someplace really nasty, like the airport terminal," Eric replied. "How about just doubling up our surgical masks?"

"Still not as good," she said, digging again and then comparing the two different types.

"That purse is a bottomless pit," Eric grinned.

"Yes, but not as good as Amazon. I should have brought more KN-95s—but of course, we weren't planning on this extended tour."

"I'm sure the hotel can direct us on where to get more," Eric said, plucking the KN-95 from her hand and putting it on. "This smells like stale bread."

"I wonder why."

"It's also like breathing though stale bread," Eric complained.

"Better than not breathing at all."

Eric pushed the stroller up to the entrance to The National Museum in Warsaw. "How much?" Eric asked, taking out his wallet.

The clerk behind the window studied him. "You sound American."

"I am."

"Not good time for tourists."

"We're not," Eric replied ruefully. "We escaped Ukraine and are waiting for flights home. Just killing time."

The woman nodded and tapped on her register. "Then you refugees. No charge."

"Really?"

"New policy. Lift spirits."

Eric glanced over at Abby whose eyes sparkled with delight. "Well, thank you," he said to the clerk. "It does help."

Eric pushed open the door for Abby. "Okay, I'm almost enjoying myself," she said as she slipped by him. "Hopefully there will be some sunny landscape painting in here to warm me up."

They wandered about, avoiding portraiture and somber still lifes. Abby turned into another wing and was greeted by a huge wilderness painting done in the grand Victorian manner, all burnished like a warm spring evening. "It's Yosemite!" she gasped. She picked Jillian up out of the stroller and walked closer, as if she would step right into it. "I'm taking you there, sweetie," she cooed. "You'll feel that mist on your face," she added, pointing to the veil catching the last rays of the sun. She lingered, pointing out things to Jillian, things she had done—stories Eric had never heard. His mother was transformed, if only for a little while. He was patient, until his stomach started to growl.

"Let's go get something to eat," he suggested. "I'm starving and our room should be ready soon."

Abby slowly turned around. He could tell she was smiling, even with her mask on. "Yes. That café—was it two blocks?" She made a motion with her hand that Eric could follow.

"The one with the yellow awning?"

"Yes. That one."

"Mom, you actually remembered where it was!"

She laughed. "Well, don't get too used to it!"

The spell lingered at a little table against a plate glass window. Outside, the yellow awning flapped against the gray sky. The waiter disappeared when Eric spoke English, but soon an older man appeared. "You like?"

"No meat, please," Abby said.

The man smiled and made an okay sign. "You?" he asked Eric. Eric didn't really care; he felt anything would taste good. He threw up his hands with a smile and the man laughed and whacked him on the back. "You *okay!*"

The meals were delicious. Eric couldn't recall his mother enjoying eating so much. When she finished she leaned back in her chair. "My goodness. You're going to have to put me in the stroller and carry Jillian."

"I think there's more room in your purse."

Abby burst out laughing. "Maybe, but it doesn't have wheels."

"Yet," Eric laughed.

When they opened the door to their room, they were greeted by two double beds, two white bathrobes hanging in the closet, and a gleaming tub in the bath. "I can't wait to get into that!" murmured Abby.

"I forgot to ask at the desk about a place to get formula and diapers," Eric replied, turning to leave again.

Abby looked over at Jillian in her stroller. "Okay, but hurry."

When Eric returned, the bathroom door was closed and he heard splashing. "Mom! Where's Jillian?"

"In here with me."

"The bath?"

"Why not? She's having a blast."

He smiled. "Well, I got diapers and formula, but no KN-95s."

"We'll make do with the regular ones. I have plenty of those. We can save the KN-95s for the airport, like you said. I'm going to wash out some clothes for Jillian and maybe for us. Do you want to add to my pile?"

"All I got is what I have on."

"Put on a robe. We'll be out of here shortly." It wasn't shortly, but Abby did eventually do the laundry and hang things all over the room to dry. They settled in for the rest of the afternoon and ordered room service for their dinner. "Well, this isn't the Yellow Awning, but what it lacks in flavor it makes up for in comfort," Abby announced, stretching out on her bed in her bathrobe.

They spent the following days eating, napping, and exploring the environs. There were other museums, but mostly they walked and admired the architecture. "You forget how old buildings are in Europe. Even back home there's such a major difference between the East Coast versus the West Coast," Abby said. "Do you remember the beautiful old buildings in New York and Boston?"

Eric shook his head. "Not really. Wasn't I about nine when we moved to California?"

"Yes. You were nine and Paige was five."

When a week had passed since their last visit to the embassy, they decided to make a trip there. The crowds were just as big so the wait was long. They were determined, though, to get an answer. When they finally got to the front of the line, the answer was not good news. No passport had arrived and they had no idea how long it would take. "Things were already difficult because of Covid," the clerk reiterated. "Now the demand is much higher."

"Do you have any idea how long?" Eric sighed.

The clerk shrugged. "Not really."

"Is there anything we could do to speed it along?" Abby asked.

"I don't know what you could do."

"Let's go, Mom." Eric and Abby pushed their way through the crowd to the outside and walked back to the hotel. Eric paid for another week before they went to their room.

They both called their respective spouses and told them the update. "There's nothing you can do?" Brian asked irritably.

"Apparently not," Abby answered.

"Well, I'm going to make a few calls."

"Is there something you want to tell me?"

"Like what?"

"Like you're really a CIA spy or something," Abby chuckled.

Brian laughed back. "Now if I was I couldn't tell you, could I?"

"Ha ha. Well, have at it."

"It can't hurt to try."

Abby got off the phone and turned to Eric. "Brian thinks he can make some calls to expedite this, but I have no idea who he thinks he's going to call."

Eric laughed. "Heather said the same thing. Well, let them make whatever calls they want. I just hope they don't mind being on hold for a week."

Abby decided to make an attempt at writing while Eric managed to get some work done. A comfortable, quiet place to work made all the difference. However, she found herself checking news outlets instead, trying to make sense out of a senseless war. "Have you heard anything from Iryna or Luka?" she asked. "How are they faring?"

"I haven't heard from Iryna," Eric replied, staring at his screen. "I guess I can take a break now and text her. I texted Luka when I crossed the border into Poland," Eric continued, "and he said I was lucky. He was still in Kyiv hearing explosions and spending some time in bomb shelters like we did. Iryna doesn't live in the heart of everything, you know."

"Most of the bombing is on the eastern and southern borders still," Abby read off her screen. "Iryna was southwest of Kyiv, right?"

"Yeah. I think so." Eric's phone pinged. "She just answered. A military base near her town was bombed, but that's it for now. She isn't sending her kids to school, though, and they did spend one night in a bomb shelter. She also says her hours have been cut at her job."

"What's her job?"

"She works in a store. I don't know what kind of store, but she says that some of the shelves are bare. They can't get supplies in."

"Oh dear. I hope she has enough money to buy food."

"Mm, Mom—we just gave her a lot of money for being a surrogate."

"Oh, yeah."

They went back to their respective computers and Abby tried a little harder to stay away from the news. It wasn't helpful to read about the atrocities that Putin was committing. Then Jillian started wailing. "Can you deal with her?" Eric asked. "I'm in the middle of something for work."

"Gladly!" Abby took her granddaughter out of the stroller where she spent almost all her time. "This poor baby never gets to kick and squirm much, strapped in like that."

"Put her on the bed. It's not like she's rolling over yet."

Abby put Jillian on the bed and she started kicking and rocking. "Hm. Maybe this hotel has cribs."

Eric looked up from his screen. "I've been so used to improvising that I didn't even think of that."

Abby smiled. "I know what you mean. I'll go down to the front desk with Jillian and ask." Abby changed the baby and took her downstairs.

"So?" Eric asked when Abby returned.

"They'll deliver one shortly. We are definitely in the lap of luxury here."

Eric laughed. "Well, compared to sleeping in a car or the hostel, I guess so."

"Thank goodness prices are so reasonable here. Hard to believe this hotel room is costing us about a quarter of what it would be in the states."

"True. The cost of this delay is miniscule compared to the cost of surrogacy."

"I know," Abby sighed. "I can help, you know. It seems like I haven't paid for much at all."

"I'll let you know when I need it."

The hotel maintenance brought in the crib and set it up. Abby put Jillian inside and she immediately closed her eyes and fell asleep. "Well, I guess she likes it."

"She likes that you're keeping her belly full," Eric replied without looking up.

Eric and Abby took a walk later on and stumbled upon the Warsaw Philharmonic. There was a rehearsal going on, so they were allowed inside. "What a building!" Eric exclaimed.

"It is gorgeous!"

"This gives the columbarium a run for its money," Eric whispered.

"Beautiful music too." They sat and listened to the rehearsal for a while until Jillian decided she was hungry and started to cry, so they hurried out. "Should we pick up something for dinner or just order from room service again."

"Let's pick something up," Eric replied. "We might as well keep pretending we're tourists."

"That's the way to make lemonade!"

29

A FEW DAYS LATER THEY FOUND THEMSELVES ONCE AGAIN WAITING IN LINE AT THE EMBASSY. The flux of Americans trying to leave had lessened considerably, but it still took a couple of hours to reach the front of the line. The clerk typed in their information and announced with apparent wonder that Jillian's passport was approved and should arrive soon. "Do you think it's safe to try to get plane tickets for the day after tomorrow?" Eric asked.

"No," the clerk replied. "I would wait until you have the passport in your hands. I'm surprised it happened this fast."

Eric and Abby exchanged glances, wondering if either Brian or Heather had actually had a hand in the matter. "Okay, thank you."

Once they were outside the noisy lobby Abby turned to Eric. "What do you think happened?"

"Heather didn't say anything when I talked to her. It must have been Brian."

"Brian didn't say anything either. Not that I'd expect him to. He was acting so secretive about it. Maybe someone will fess up once we tell them the news."

"Should we pay for the room day by day?"

"I don't know," Abby mused. "What if it's rented out from under us?"

"I'll tell the front desk the situation and see what they say." They stopped at a restaurant where Eric got a sausage and sauerkraut sandwich while Abby got her usual salad. Eric went to the front desk and Abby took Jillian to the room. "Can we be assured of keeping the room if we pay day-by-day? We don't know when the baby's passport will get here."

"You should pay for a week. We can reimburse you if you don't stay. There is a twenty-four hour cancellation notice time, so we would have to charge you for one extra night if you don't give us twenty-four hours."

Eric shrugged. "Okay." He paid for another week and went up to the room. Abby was burping Jillian when he entered. "I had to pay for a week again. But if we leave in a hurry, we would only have to pay for one night that we're not here because of their policy. They'll refund us the rest."

"That's not bad and at least we won't be out on the street again. Anyway, I called Brian. Apparently he does know people in high places. Or at least knows people who know people in high places."

"Who?" Eric asked with interest.

"He wouldn't tell me. He just said that someone owed him a favor and that person started making calls. That's all he would say."

Eric looked at his mother skeptically. "Why won't he tell you?"

"Come on, Eric," Abby replied, rolling her eyes. "It was a favor. They're not supposed to see the light of day. It would probably force whomever into an arena of accusations or even cause them to lose their job."

Eric laughed. "I could see you doing something like that, but not Brian."

"I now see that I've been less than an ideal role model," Abby sighed dramatically, "but desperate times call for desperate measures."

"You're just full of clichés."

"Can't help it," Abby sighed again. "I used to read Bartlett's Familiar Quotations for fun as a child."

"You're an enigma, Mom."

"I believe the school board told me that once. I took it as a compliment."

"I'm sure you did," Eric chuckled.

"So . . . do you think the embassy will call when the passport arrives or do we have to keep checking every day?"

"Mom. One thing you taught me is never to wait for people to call."

"That's right. The squeaky wheel . . ."

Eric groaned. "We'll go again tomorrow. And now I have some work to do."

"Okay. I'll leave you be."

The next morning they woke up and looked out the window at a rather heavy snowstorm. "We can't take Jillian out in this," Eric mused.

"Does she need to be there to pick up the passport?"

"I don't know. It seems like she doesn't. They already know that she exists."

"I'd just hate the idea of getting hung up in another glitch because we didn't bring her."

"I'll go. If the passport is there and she needs to come, I'll get an Uber for you and you can bring her." Eric left and Abby turned on iTunes. She danced around the room with Jillian, enjoying the reggae rhythm and the giggles coming from the baby. She played peek-a-boo and tried to remember the words to children's songs, but most of the words escaped her. She put Jillian back in the crib and searched for nursery rhyme books on her Kindle so she could refresh her memory.

Eric finally returned. "Any luck?" Abby asked, putting her Kindle down.

"Nope. But the clerk said Jillian doesn't need to be present for us to pick up the passport and not to bother coming in every day, just call. Shall we attempt to sightsee?"

"Is there anything within walking distance we haven't already seen?"

"Well, I imagine."

"I'd rather not today," Abby said glancing out the window. "Jillian and I got our exercise by dancing around the room. I think I'll try to write now."

"Okay. I always have work to do, too."

Eric called every day about the passport and finally a few days later it had arrived. It was fairly late in the day when Eric was able to pick up the passport. "You got this pretty quickly," the clerk said.

Eric just nodded. "Do you have any suggestions on how to get a plane ticket?" he asked at the embassy.

"No. I really don't. It's terribly impacted."

Eric got back to the hotel and told them that they'd be leaving the following day. He spent a couple of hours on the phone trying to get plane tickets, but there was nothing available. "Well, I guess we just go to the airport and try."

"I suppose we'll need another Covid test," Abby sighed.

"I wonder if the testing site at the airport is open early." He did some searching on his phone. "They open at eight."

"We'll be the first in line!" They ordered room service and went to bed.

They were indeed first in line for the Covid tests, but not for the ticket counter. There were hordes of people as usual. They stood on line for a couple of hours before getting to the counter and facing the very harried agent. "There is nothing and many people waiting," she said wearily.

Abby leaned forward. "Do you honestly think there is any point in waiting here?"

"No," sighed the agent. "Maybe try a different airport."

"Like where?"

"Frankfurt. There are trains."

"How long would it take?"

She shrugged. "Driving ten hours. I don't know about train."

Eric started tapping on his phone. "Not that much longer by transit," he said. "Twelve or thirteen hours." He turned to the agent. "Where is the train station?"

"Short walk," she pointed.

"Thanks." Eric and Abby went to a corner to discuss what to do. "I think it's a good idea to take the train to Frankfurt. What do you think?"

Abby exhaled sharply. "I thought we were finally on the last leg of this ordeal. Now we have another half day postponement."

"Would you prefer sitting in the airport for who knows how many days?"

"No. You're right. We need to go to the train station. But let's take care of all our needs here before we go . . . just in case. So far, nothing has gone smoothly." They took turns using the restroom, fed and changed Jillian, checked their supply of diapers and formula and bought a couple of bottles of water.

"Shall we?" Eric said, taking Abby's elbow.

They started walking in the direction the agent had pointed and Eric scrolled through the map app. "Are we going in the right direction?" Abby asked as they trudged down slushy sidewalks.

"Yeah. It's not far at all." They got to the train station and Eric went to the agent there while Abby sat down with Jillian. "Well, we have a bit of a wait, but we have tickets for Frankfurt."

"When does the train leave?"

"A couple of hours."

"When are we supposed to get to the Frankfurt Airport?"

"The middle of the night, I'm afraid."

"And then what will we do?"

"Wait at the airport and try to get on a flight to the states."

"I don't even care where we wind up, just somewhere in America where we can get a flight to San Francisco."

Jillian slept, Abby read, and Eric did some work on his computer. The end was in sight. They were confident that they would be home in a couple of days. "Maybe we should try to keep Jillian awake so we can all sleep on the train?" Abby asked, taking her out of the stroller.

"How are you planning on keeping her awake?"

"Singing and dancing, of course."

"In the train station?"

"Why not?"

"Because soon there will be no room left on the floor," he replied, nodding to a fresh horde of people coming through the doors. "We'd better stick real close together."

"My God," murmured Abby. Like a flood, the people swirled around, filling every void. "At least we have tickets."

- - -

"I don't think that's going to stop anyone from trying to get on."

Finally an announcement was made—in Polish, of course. The time seemed right, though, so they gathered their things and followed the crowd. "I hope this is the right train," Eric puffed as he pushed forward.

"Is this the train to Frankfurt?" shouted Abby, hoping someone would understand her. She repeated her cry as they got pushed around. Then she noticed someone nodding at her and pointing ahead. She smiled and waved. Eventually they scrambled to one of the last two seats side by side.

"Throw yourself on them!" gasped Eric. "I've got to stow this stroller."

"And what about Jillian?" yelled Abby. "Do I toss her, too?"

"Oh, you know what I mean!" Eric managed to squeeze the flattened stroller on top of some flattened cardboard boxes and then pushed Abby to the window. "Can you hold her for a while? I'm bushed."

"Yes, of course," she replied, putting her purse between them and balancing Jillian on her lap.

"Here are the tickets, in case I'm asleep when the conductor comes around."

The train jerked, indicating it was starting to leave the station, and the passengers were at a fever pitch. Abby tucked the tickets into her purse. The rhythm of the train sounds increased, drowning out the passengers. Or maybe they were just quieting down, now as relieved as she was that they were leaving Warsaw behind. She felt strangely relaxed, rocked by the train. Her eyelids drooped, so she looked over at Eric to keep herself awake. He was already asleep, his mouth wide open.

30

THE RUMBLE OF THE TRAIN MUFFLED THE SOUND OF THE CRYING CHILDREN. Mothers sat stone faced, eyes bright with unshed tears. Others were slumped over, asleep. Eric and Abby took turns holding Jillian who in turns, napped or lay contentedly in their lap, watching what was going on around her. "I suppose they'll want to look at our passports as we cross the border," Abby mentioned offhandedly.

"I guess," Eric replied. But they crossed the border into Germany and no one came around asking for them. "Well," Eric finally said, "They've probably suspended inspecting them because of all the refugees. You can imagine how tedious that would be."

"Let alone the responsibility of what to do with all the passengers who don't have one," Abby mused, looking around. "I'm sure it's more than just the usual few." She then sighed. "Will we have to get another Covid test at the airport in Frankfurt?"

"Maybe not if we get on a plane right away. Didn't they say they were good for forty-eight hours?"

"I can't keep track anymore. Between testing and masking and vaccinations . . . it's hard to know what to do anymore."

"Just have to be vigilant."

"Kind of hard to be when you're hungry," Abby replied. "I wonder if there's a dining car on this train."

"That would be kind of awkward with Jillian," Eric frowned. "Let's just wait until we get to the airport."

"Mm," Abby retorted. "Remember that endless, foodless night at the Istanbul airport?"

"Maybe there will be a pretzel kiosk. I know you love those big German pretzels," Eric smiled.

"At this point I'd probably eat a McDonald's hamburger! I'm that hungry."

Eric reached in his backpack and took out a granola bar. "Here — it's the last one."

"What will you eat, then?"

"You're the one who said you were hungry. I'm fine."

"Thanks."

They took turns playing with Jillian as they had to change trains a few times. Dozing seemed out of the question for more than a few minutes at a time. They finally got to Frankfurt in the wee hours of the morning. They hustled off the train and started walking to the airport terminal. Luckily it was a short walk. "I doubt the airport would be crowded at this hour," Eric said, but he was quite wrong. The lines at the ticket counter were long.

"Oh no," groaned Abby. "Here we go again." She fussed and started doing an inpatient little dance as she studied the floor. "Do you see an ATM?"

"Over there. Why?"

"I have an idea." She left the line and went to the ATM. When she returned she asked Eric, "How much is three hundred Euros in American dollars?"

Eric looked at his phone. "About three hundred twenty-five dollars. Again . . . why?"

"I'm going to try to get us on a plane the old-fashioned way."

Eric looked at her curiously. "Huh?"

"Shhh," Abby retorted, tapping a ticket envelope against the palm of her hand.

"Where did you get that?" Eric asked.

"The floor."

"Ew."

"Desperate times—"

"I know, I know."

After more than an hour and a half, they finally reached the ticket counter. "Let me," Abby said, pushing in front of Eric. "Do you speak English?"

"Yes," the agent replied.

"We are Americans coming from Ukraine with a tiny, newborn baby. We need to get home to San Francisco, but we are willing to land anywhere in the U.S. first." The agent automatically reached for the ticket folder. "Don't open that!" she hissed.

"But—"

"It's for you," Abby continued tersely.

The agent looked down at the envelope and then back at Abby. "Me?" the clerk whispered.

"Yes. For your trouble."

The agent turned the envelope over and sighed. "I'm glad the back is filled out," she said clearly. "Makes my job easier than having to look through the tickets." She studied the back as she typed and after a while, Abby realized the agent was merely acting out business as usual for the security cameras. She hadn't really considered the possibility of cameras; she just didn't want to draw attention. Abby started to shake.

"I-I didn't think-" Abby faltered.

"Oh, I know," the agent replied loudly, brightly. "It's just impossible to find seats." She typed again for a few minutes and then said, "I just got a cancellation in business class. I can charge the difference on your card."

"Of course," Abby managed to say.

"So—if I could just see your card and identification so I know it's you."

"Yes." Abby started digging through her purse, found her wallet and produced the desired items.

"Okay then," the agent said as she finished typing. "That's two seats and a bassinet in business class to Los Angeles—"

"We'll take them!" Eric interjected.

The agent managed a laugh. "And here are your new tickets. Your flight leaves in a couple of hours at Gate 37. Oh, I forgot. Do you have your Covid tests?"

"Oh, back in Warsaw we—"

"Got it, Mom," Eric said whipping out his phone. He pulled up their test results and the agent looked at them perfunctorily.

"Excellent," the agent said, handing over the tickets. "Thank you for your patience." The agent then casually slipped the envelope Abby had presented under the counter.

"Thank *you*," Abby breathed. She turned away and got beyond the line of people waiting before stopping and grabbing Eric's arm.

"Are you okay, Mom?"

"Yes. I just need something to eat."

"I think you're suffering from more than that," Eric replied, grinning. "I think you're just coming off the performance of a lifetime."

Abby managed to bow slightly and then breathed deeply. "Thank you."

"I don't know how you did it."

"Naivety helped a lot," Abby sighed. "At least at first."

"Let's celebrate by getting something to eat."

But, as Abby predicted, there weren't any open restaurants. A coffee kiosk, however, had dubious looking pre-wrapped sandwiches that everyone seemed to be eating. "We better grab one," Abby said, "in case the flight is delayed. At least we'll get a meal on the plane."

They took their sandwiches to the waiting area near their gate and started taking them apart to make one edible for Abby. She took a big blissful bite. "This time we really made it," she sighed. "And in business class, no less."

"Don't jinx it!" Eric scolded.

"I know, but at least we have tickets," Abby replied. Then she lifted her sandwich. "Here's to bribery!"

"Hear, hear!" cried Eric. "Oh, I better call Heather."

"And I better call Brian. What time is it back home?"

"Oh . . ." Eric glanced at his phone. "Maybe after eleven or midnight."

"Let's just text, then. Brian hasn't been up past eleven in years."

Abby tapped out a message with one finger as she finished her sandwich. "I just realized I can't give him an ETA because we don't have a flight from LAX to SFO. Maybe we should get back in line."

"We haven't got time for that, thank God," Eric muttered. "We shouldn't have a hard time getting a flight from Los Angeles."

"I don't know, with Covid and all."

"Then we'll rent a car."

Abby looked at him dubiously. "I don't think either one of us will be in any condition to drive for six hours."

"After sleeping in business class for how many hours?"

"Okay, okay," Abby replied, taking a deep breath. "I don't want to think about it, really."

"Me neither."

They tried to keep Jillian awake as they waited. Since there would be a bassinet in business class, they would both get a chance to sleep provided she slept on the plane. They bounced her, sang to her, played peek-a-boo, but she started to fuss. "Why haven't they announced pre-boarding for our flight?" Abby asked. "It's scheduled to leave in fifteen minutes."

"You didn't really expect everything to go smoothly, did you?" Eric smirked.

They watched the clock and another half hour went by. Finally an announcement came over the speaker that it would be two more hours before boarding. "Let's hope it's only two hours," Abby added.

But it wasn't. They roamed the airport, bought candy to snack on, fed and diapered Jillian, used the restroom . . . finally an announcement. They could start boarding. Because they were business class and they had a baby, they were one of the first to board. But that only meant they had to sit on the plane while everyone else got on and settled in. It was another forty-five minutes before the plane finally took off. The most annoying part was that the flight time itself was less than two hours. "Sorry mom, but this flight is too short to get a meal. We'll have to wait until the flight from London to Los Angeles to eat."

"I think I'm so hungry that I'm not anymore. Does that make sense?"

Eric laughed. "As much sense as anything else that's happening."

The flight to London was fast and smooth and they were even able to get a little shuteye. Even better, they didn't have too long to wait at Heathrow before boarding the next flight to Los Angeles. When they got on that plane, they hugged each other and Jillian. They texted Brian and Heather and settled into their seats. The flight attendant came around. "I'm taking meal orders," she began.

"I'm a vegetarian," Abby replied, then grinned. "But I'm starving!"

"I'll bring you a lovely cheese and fruit plate. Any requirements for you, sir?"

"Nope. I want all the food I can get! I don't care what it is!"

The flight attendant chuckled. "I'll bring you a hearty British meal to remember your time in England."

Abby opened her mouth to correct the flight attendant. "We're actually not coming from England," she began.

"Oh, if it had only been that easy!" Eric ribbed Abby before she could launch into one of her lengthy explanations. "Thank you." The attendant moved on and Eric looked over at Abby. "I had to stop you before you got to the part about you stuffing the ticket envelope with—
—"

"Shhh!" Abby glared. "I wouldn't have told her that."

"Probably not," Eric grinned. "She would have had to go on her break long before then."

Abby stuck out her tongue. The plane began taxiing and several minutes later, it shot into the sky. As the plane leveled off, Jillian fell asleep in her bassinet and both Eric and Abby reclined in their luxurious seats. When the flight attendant came with their meals, they were both snoring.

31

JILLIAN'S WAILING WOKE THEM BOTH. "Oh," moaned Abby. "How long have we been sleeping?"

"I don't know," mumbled Eric as he reached over for Jillian, "but we didn't get our meals."

"Guess we needed sleep more than food," Abby yawned.

"Tell my growling stomach that. Can you get my backpack overhead?"

As Abby reached she glanced at her watch. "Whoa. It looks like we slept for three hours."

"Feels like it," Eric replied. "Now take Jillian. I'm going to take this packet and a bottle and find an attendant. Might as well use this formula sample." Eric rummaged through his backpack and found the bottle. "Ugh," he muttered. "I thought I cleaned this."

"And how many days and countries ago was that?" muttered Abby. "They must have premixed bottles on board—and we probably won't even have to pay for them."

Eric frowned and left with the bottle. He returned a couple of minutes later without it. "You're right. Jillian gets a free meal, and they'll bring ours shortly."

"Wonderful," sighed Abby. "Feels like smooth sailing from now on, don't you think?"

"I'm not taking anything for granted," Eric replied coolly. "You were the one wondering how we were going to get from Los Angeles to San Francisco just a few hours ago." He sat down. "Did you let Brian know when our flight arrives in LA?"

"Yes, but I also told him not to hold his breath."

Eric grinned. "I told Heather the same thing."

Abby chuckled. "But first things first," she added, putting down her tray in anticipation of the first real meal she's had in days. Soon the attendant arrived with a cart and handed her a fruit and cheese plate and Eric a platter of fish and chips.

"And don't be afraid to ask for more," smiled the attendant.

Nothing was said between them for several minutes as they stuffed their mouths with good food. Finally Eric managed a garbled, "How's yours?"

"Can't you tell?" Abby laughed, passing a hand over her nearly empty plate. "I'm afraid I may take her up on her offer."

"Why not? Can't a lady have two fruit and cheese plates?"

"This one can!" So they both had seconds.

After Jillian was fed Abby walked her up and down the aisle. She stopped several times as people fussed over the baby, but was careful not to get too close. "Gosh, you'd think they'd know better with Covid and all," Abby said as she sat down and adjusted her mask. "Everyone wanted to paw at her."

"Ah, the promise of new life," Eric replied. "If we don't get Covid after all we've been through, I think our immune systems are impervious."

Abby laughed. "Guess that's true. Funny, I hadn't started worrying about it again until we were more relaxed."

"War will do that to you!"

"It did feel a bit like life and death, didn't it?"

Eric just nodded. Jillian yawned, so he put her back in her bassinet and then took out his computer. "Might as well take advantage of the free Wi-Fi and do some work."

"It's either that or go into a food coma," Abby said, reaching for her own computer. "Although I don't know how you can switch gears so easily." She thought she might wander off into social media, but instead opened Word and started typing. After a while, her speed caught Eric's attention.

"Speaking of shifting gears, I think you're in overdrive."

"I'm just so behind on documenting this trip," Abby replied with a sigh. "I want to make sure Jillian has something written about her perilous journey home."

"Ah, just like that—from trip to perilous journey. Apparently you're writing a book."

"Maybe," Abby replied, staring at her screen. "Now be quiet."

"Yes ma'am."

They continued working while Jillian slept in the bassinet. All sense of time was lost on them until the plane made a sudden dip. Abby looked up and noticed the windows were dark gray and streaked with wet snow. Then the plane jerked and wobbled. "O-oh!" Abby exclaimed, looking over at Eric. Another dip and sway and she reached out for his arm. A chime sounded and the fasten seatbelts light went on overhead.

"We've come into some heavy turbulence," announced the pilot. "Please return to your seat, secure your belongings, and fasten your seatbelts."

"I guess our belongings include Jillian," Abby said as she hastily stowed her phone and their computers into her purse and pulled on her seatbelt. Eric was already taking Jillian out of her bassinet. He put his arms around her tightly as the plane swerved and dipped. "This is scary!" Abby blurted out.

Eric somehow reached out his hand and grabbed hers. "It's alright. Just a bad storm."

The rumbling and rattling of the plane didn't quite drown out Jillian's screams. The din was pierced here and there by suddenly unrepressed exclamations from the passengers. The pilot announced for the attendants to take their seats, but they already had. In economy class an overhead bin burst open, causing a new round of shrieks from the back of the plane.

"Okay," Eric gritted his teeth. "A *really* bad storm."

Abby glanced over at him and wished she hadn't. He was deathly white. The engines roared as the pilot pushed the plane higher and slowly but steadily, the turbulence decreased into the normal range. As the roaring faded the voices started rising like a thousand startled birds. "I think I can breathe now," Abby finally gasped, taking her hand from Eric's.

"Beats anything at Disneyland," Eric said, bending down to kiss Jillian's head.

Above the chatter was an insistent voice back over the wing section that was joined by two or three more. A couple of attendants got up to see when the pilot came on again, "We'll need to make an emergency landing in Moncton, New Brunswick. Please stay seated with your seatbelts fastened."

Again the sound startled cries from panicked passengers. "Oh my God!" burst Abby. "What's wrong?!"

"Well, nothing horrible if we're landing in Moncton," Eric replied matter-of-factly. "At least we're not landing in the Atlantic."

Abby glared at him. "You would have to mention that! And where the hell is Moncton?!"

"Canada. Maybe we can rent a car—" Abby whacked his arm. "No!"

"Just hold my hand and calm down."

The plane pitched forward into a steep descent. Again there was turbulence, but nothing like they had experienced minutes earlier. There was no sound above the roar of the engines and the rattles and rumbles of the plane. It seemed to Abby that everyone clutched the arms of their seats or the hands of the person sitting next to them. She could see that even the flight attendants sitting in their seats looked a bit anxious. Eric found himself hugging Jillian tighter to his chest as Abby's hand slipped to his elbow.

The plane descended quickly and finally touched the ground, bumping up and down as well as veering side to side as it taxied. It stopped and the flight attendants jumped up to open the doors and inflate the evacuation ramps. Somehow they managed a pretty orderly emergency exit and soon Eric and Abby leapt onto the ramps. Eric held Jillian close to him, and Abby did the same with her purse. People picked themselves up at the bottom of the ramp and ran every which way through the heavy snowfall. Someone ran out from the terminal and directed them inside while the crew made sure the plane was empty and took up the herding from the rear.

They got inside the building and stood around, breathing heavily, while Eric tried to calm Jillian. "Everyone is off!" one of the pilots yelled and that brought a loud round of applause.

The shock wore off after several minutes and people started murmuring among themselves. "I hope you weren't attached to anything in your backpack," Abby said.

"Some paperwork but my manager probably has copies," Eric replied. "Of course, I should get it back eventually, but there were a couple of premix formula bottles in there, too.

"Great," sighed Abby. "Well, there should be something here at the airport." She then fished around in her purse and eventually produced her phone. "Yet again—we'd better call Brian and let him know what's happening."

"Go ahead and text them both and tell Heather I'll call her later when we know more."

Abby tapped for a while. "I guess we can cross New Brunswick off our bucket list."

"Was it on yours?"

"No. I'm not even sure where New Brunswick is."

"It's just above Maine. West of Nova Scotia."

"I knew it was somewhere out there." She looked out the windows at the dreary winter beyond. "I wonder what's going to happen now. Will they put us up in a hotel or just try to get us all on another flight?"

"This is a lot of people to put on another plane to Los Angeles."

"So then they should be happy to get us on a flight directly to San Francisco from here."

"Well, that would be nice but we'll just have to wait and see what happens next. There are some empty seats over there if you want to sit," he added.

"I don't know. I'm too restless to sit. What are we going to do about feeding Jillian?"

Eric looked around. "No idea."

"This is even worse than being in Ukraine, Poland and Germany. At least we had the diapers and formula there."

"Well, that's not how I remember it," Eric sighed, but Abby was too distracted to argue. They stood around quietly for a while, waiting for some kind of information about what was going to happen to them. "That empty spot is still there." Eric pointed to a place in the corner of the room. "Let's sit down."

They pushed through the crowd to the corner of the room. Jillian was restless and whimpering. "We've got to get her some food," Abby said. "Maybe one of our flight attendants would know about this airport. I just saw one."

"It's worth a try."

Abby shoved through the crowd again and found someone in a flight attendant's uniform. "We had formula for the baby on the plane. Do you think there's somewhere in the airport that sells it?"

"Sorry, but I don't know this airport," the attendant frowned thoughtfully. "I'd try to help, but I have to stay here with the passengers. See if you can find an information desk."

Abby started walking through the mostly deserted terminal. She did find what looked like a welcome center, but no one was there. Finally she came across a couple of stores that were open, but none had baby items and none of the clerks had any helpful ideas on what she should do. She started to walk back to where she had left

Eric and Jillian, quietly cursing the Covid shutdown and trying to devise a plan to get the backpack off the plane. Just as she started to give up all hope for any way to feed Jillian, she saw a woman pushing a stroller. She gathered up all her New York chutzpah and went up to the woman. "Hello," she said. "Beautiful baby." Abby looked into the stroller and saw that the baby was a few months old.

"Thank you."

"We were on the plane that made an emergency landing. Were you?"

"No. I just got here. I'm glad you're okay. That must have been scary."

"Very!" Abby exclaimed. "And we have a three week old baby with us."

"Oh my!" the woman exclaimed sympathetically. "That's terrible."

Abby inhaled deeply. "We had to leave our things on the plane, so we have no food for the baby. I haven't been able to find any formula here—would you happen to have any to spare? I do have a bottle in my purse."

The woman shook her head. "Sorry, no. I'm breastfeeding."

Abby's face dropped and no matter how hard she tried, she couldn't hide it. "Oh," she finally said.

"Well," the woman hesitated, "being an emergency and all maybe I could express some breast milk for you."

Abby spontaneously hugged the woman. "That would be wonderful! Thank you!"

The woman pulled back and smiled. "Let's find a restroom."

They found one nearby and went inside. "I can watch your baby if you want privacy," Abby said as she rummaged through her purse. "Oh damn! I don't have a bottle. It must have been the one in Eric's backpack."

"Your husband?"

"Oh, you flatter," gushed Abby. "The baby is my granddaughter. Eric is my son."

"I see," the woman replied with a smile. "It's complicated."

"I can breastfeed her if that's okay with you."

"Oh my God, you're amazing! Thank you so much." Then Abby wavered. Was this woman healthy? Was she a drug user? But what choice did she have? Jillian needed to eat. "Oh my," Abby replied. "You're a gift from heaven. What's your name?"

"Olivia. And this is Liam."

"He's so handsome," Abby said, looking down at him as they exited the restroom. "My name is Abby and soon you'll meet Jillian."

"Just show me the way," Olivia replied as she pushed her stroller along. "Where are you from?"

"California, but we came from Ukraine. Jillian is a surrogate—"

"So many wows!" gasped Olivia. "You escaped the war and—well, it's an honor."

"No, no—I'm giving you the medal," Abby laughed. "Are you coming or going somewhere?"

"Neither. I was just picking up my husband, but it appears his flight was delayed. The weather and all . . ."

Abby gave Olivia a very brief overview of their adventures as they crossed the terminal. Up ahead stood Eric, holding a very cranky Jillian. "This angel here is named Olivia," Abby announced, "and she's going to breastfeed Jillian."

"She is?" Eric replied incredulously. Olivia laughed. "I mean, well, that's—great!"

"Is it possible to meet under stranger circumstances?" smiled Olivia. "Not that it should be, but well, you know—"

"Not a drop of formula in this joint," Abby explained, "and then I bumped into Olivia."

"Well," Eric said, relaxing a little. "I thank you. Desperate times call for desperate measures." He glanced over at his mother just in time to see her roll her eyes. "I just hope Jillian is nice about it."

"It'll be fine. Let's go find a quiet spot, Abby."

Abby took Jillian and Olivia pushed the stroller over to a far row of empty seats that faced a wall. She unbuttoned her blouse and produced a breast. Abby handed Jillian over and then took off her coat to give Olivia some extra privacy. However, Jillian started hollering when covered in stuffy darkness. "She's not used to being covered while feeding," Abby said.

"I don't need to be covered, anyway," Olivia replied. "If people are curious enough to come over here only to be offended, so what?"

"Of course," Abby replied meekly. As she put her jacket back on, Liam started crying and she was happy for the distraction. "Oh, who's a big boy?" she asked as she picked him up out of the stroller. Liam looked at her suspiciously. "Why are you looking at me like that?" Abby baby-talked. "Your mommy thought I looked her age." Liam started laughing. "Oh, you're a comedian . . ."

About fifteen minutes later Olivia announced that Jillian seemed to be done for now. Abby took Jillian and Olivia buttoned up and then they all strolled back to Eric. "Jillian's a natural," Olivia said to Eric. "Very polite."

"Glad to hear it," Eric smiled. "I'm sure it did her some good."

"I'm sure it did, too," Olivia affirmed. "Now I'm going to go off somewhere quiet. Liam is acting tired and it seems like it's going to be a long wait. But if I see you around in a couple of hours, I can try another feeding."

"Thank you," Eric replied, taking Jillian from Abby. "That's very kind of you."

"I'm glad to help. You've been through a lot."

"Thank you. You're a dear," Abby said, patting Olivia's shoulder as she turned away. They watched her disappear into an empty concourse. "I guess Canadians are as nice as they say," she murmured.

32

A UNIFORMED AGENT CLIMBED UP ON A CHAIR AND ADDRESSED THE STRANDED TRAVELERS. "A plane is being flown in to continue your flight to Los Angeles. Unfortunately the snowstorm is causing delays throughout the northeast, so we do not have an estimated time for its arrival here in Moncton or its arrival in Los Angeles." The latter was received with innumerable groans and mumblings.

"What about our luggage?" someone shouted.

"It has been unloaded and will be with you on the next flight."

"What about the overhead bins?" Eric asked.

"We're double checking the cabin and we'll have a call for items left behind once we're sure everything has been removed."

"I hope I can give a positive identification," mumbled Eric. "I guess the company paperwork in my backpack ought to do."

"You said that there wasn't anything terribly important in your backpack."

"I want it all back, though."

"Ask them if we can get a flight to San Francisco instead of Los Angeles," Abby said.

"Mom, do you see any flights to San Francisco on the boards?"

Abby glanced around. "No. But it doesn't hurt to ask."

"No, but it complicates things."

"Fine!" Abby snapped. "I'll ask myself!" Abby hitched Jillian up on her hip and marched over to the man who just spoke. "Is there a flight to San Francisco? We're traveling with this three-week-old baby and that's actually our final destination, not Los Angeles."

The agent looked more at Jillian than Abby. "This carrier doesn't go from here to San Francisco directly. Another carrier might, but with this storm, you're likely to have the same delays. You could ask at the airport's information desk."

"I've already been there, looking for formula for this baby!" The agent leaned back against Abby's onslaught. "There's no one there!"

The agent blinked. "I'm sorry. Covid, you know—"

"Oh!" Abby scoffed.

"Another thing to consider," the agent sighed, "is that you'll likely not get a full refund for stepping away from this flight."

"So we're all just prisoners here!" Abby huffed.

"Yes, *we* are," the agent replied. She could tell by the crinkle around his eyes that he was smiling behind his mask.

"Thank you." Abby turned on her heels and marched back to Eric. "You're right," she muttered.

They passed the time on their phones and playing with Jillian. Finally it was announced that items left in the cabin could be claimed at gate twelve. Eric returned with his backpack and immediately opened it to remove a diaper. "I'll take her to the ladies' room," Abby announced. "At least there's hot water, paper towels and a changing table in there."

"Might as well not make everyone around us more miserable," Eric grinned. "Here's some ointment for diaper rash."

"Thanks," Abby replied. "Have you seen Olivia?"

"No."

"Maybe I'll run into her on the way to the ladies' room. Jillian is going to need another feeding."

While Abby was away Eric emptied his backpack and tried to make some order of the contents. There were some surprises, including a smashed granola bar and a bottle of premixed formula. "Ta da!" he said as Abby returned with Jillian.

"Where did you get that?"

"It was sandwiched between some diapers," Eric explained. "Apparently your purse and my backpack are competing with one another."

"Well, thank goodness because I didn't see Olivia anywhere. We even took a little walk, looking for her."

Eric looked at the label. "I guess it should be alright. It's all in German."

Abby shook her head. "That would have come in handy how many times? Next time we do this—"

"You're joking, right?"

Abby chuckled. "Right. Next time let's get a baby straight from the cabbage patch."

"Huh?"

"You never heard the old saying that a baby was found in the cabbage patch? Like a flying stork?"

"No. Thus Cabbage Patch dolls, I presume. God those dolls were ugly," Eric sniffed. "Didn't Paige have one?"

"She did. Am I feeding or are you?"

"I am," Eric replied, reaching for Jillian.

Abby handed Jillian over. "I'm going to look for something for us to snack on."

"Thanks," Eric said, as he positioned the bottle. "And look for something other than a granola bar."

"I'll do my best," she smiled.

Eric was about finished feeding Jillian when it was announced that their plane just landed and was taxiing towards the terminal. Conditions had improved and they'd be boarding in about forty-five minutes. Abby came rushing up and tossed him a flat box. "Did I hear right?" she panted.

"Yes, we should be leaving soon." Eric turned the box over. "Russell Stover?"

"I think everyone has stripped the gift shop," Abby sighed, dropping into a seat. "Not even a piece of jerky left for you. At least it's mixed nuts, so there's some protein."

"And chocolate!" Eric grinned.

"Yes, chocolate—" she grabbed the box and started peeling off the cellophane. She lifted the lid and popped one in her mouth. "Mm!"

They both ate several pieces as they texted their spouses the latest flight news. "What time do you think we'll be landing in LA?" Abby asked, wiping her screen with her sleeve.

"In about nine or ten hours," Eric replied. "Depending if we have a stop or not, though I doubt we do."

Abby looked at her watch. "What time zone are we in?"

"Atlantic so four hours ahead."

"Damn. So we'll arrive in the middle of the night in Los Angeles?"

"Well, it'll be about four. There's probably a six o'clock flight from LA to San Francisco or Oakland. That's not too long a wait."

"I guess it doesn't matter. I mean . . . what else can go wrong?"

Eric rolled his eyes. "I'm sure the fates will come up with something. They've done very well so far."

Abby looked up at the ceiling. "Have mercy!"

The plane was older and smaller, so there were no business class amenities. They took turns holding Jillian and dozing. A box type sandwich lunch stood in for a meal, of which Eric ate both and Abby got by on apples, crackers, and a couple of yogurts—and their chocolates, of course. There was a premix formula bottle for Jillian, although they were charged for it. The flight went smoothly and they landed in Los Angeles just as expected at four. Due to the early hour and the pandemic LAX was particularly deserted. They went through customs and then headed to the ticket counter. "When is the next flight to San Francisco?" Eric asked.

The agent looked at her computer. "Six-thirty."

"Two seats, please. And we have a baby."

"Sorry. I only have one seat left."

"Goddammit!" Eric's voice echoed through the terminal and the few people there turned and stared. "Sorry," he muttered, a blush rising above his mask. "It's just that this trip has been endless."

"I'm sorry to hear that. I can put you on standby."

"Do that, I guess, but when is the next flight with two seats?"

"Eight-thirty."

"Can you give me two seats on that flight and then cancel if we get on the earlier one?"

"Yes sir." He took out his credit card, wondering how much all this would cost. He had a lot of phone calling to do when they got home to untangle all the connections and make sure he wasn't overcharged."

"Well," Eric said when he plopped down next to Abby. "As expected, we're not done yet with problematic travel."

"What now?"

"There's only one seat left on the six-thirty flight. We have tickets for eight-thirty and on standby for the six-thirty."

"Why don't you and Jillian take the seat on the six-thirty one? I'll wait for the eight-thirty. She needs to get home."

"No, Mom. You've been a big help and we're going to stay together."

Abby shrugged. "Okay. I guess we can't call Brian and Heather yet since we don't know what flight we'll be on."

Eric exhaled. "I guess not."

"Shall we go to the gate and wait?"

"I suppose. There's no point staying here at the ticket counter."

They went through the security line and sat down at the gate. There was no one at the booth yet and no one even waiting. They fed and changed Jillian and waited, bouncing Jillian to keep her happy. Finally people started showing up and the booth opened up. Eric went up to speak to the agent. "Let me see what I can do," the agent winked at Eric.

"Uh, okay. Thanks." Eric returned to the waiting area.

"Did you tell her what we've been through?" Abby asked. "And that we have a baby with us?"

"Yes, Mom," he sighed. "She said he'd see what she could do. And then she winked at me."

- - -

"Ooh," Abby laughed. "That's a good sign."

Several passengers went up to the booth and Eric noticed that the agent looked at him when she picked up the phone. When the agent was finished with the call, she waved to Eric to come over. "I have good news. That young man over there is giving up his seat for you."

"Oh man!" Eric cried out, turning to see who the agent was motioning to. "That's wonderful of him."

"Aw," shrugged the agent. "He gets a free flight. You just need to know who'll take the bait."

"I still need to thank him." As Eric turned away the agent cleared her throat. Eric looked back. "And thank you too, of course."

"Certainly, but I do need to print your boarding passes."

Eric chuckled with embarrassment. "That would help."

After Eric got the passes, he went over to talk to the young man for a minute before returning to where Abby was sitting. "Are we good to go on the six-thirty?" she asked.

"Yep. Thanks to that young man I was talking to."

Abby smiled and waved at the man who did the same in return. "He certainly seems friendly."

"Oh, he is. He's in no hurry to get anywhere and now he has a free flight *and* a breakfast date with the agent when her shift ends."

Abby laughed. "He told you that?"

"Yeah, Eric replied. "He pretty much thanked *me.*"

Abby looked over at the young man, but he was busy making eyes at the agent. "Well, it's going to be a good day for everyone."

33

"FINALLY SOMETHING WENT THE WAY IT WAS SUPPOSED TO," ABBY SIGHED AS THEY DISEMBARKED AT SAN FRANCISCO INTERNATIONAL AIRPORT.

"Shhh!" Eric hissed, shifting Jillian from one arm to the other. "I'm not celebrating until I'm home in bed!"

They hurried to baggage claim, if only because it was the logical place to meet someone. But no one was there. They looked around anxiously. "Are they stuck in traffic?" Abby wondered aloud.

Eric groaned. "Did you text Heather?"

"No."

"I forgot to. I guess I was distracted by that dating game at LAX."

"Did you—" Abby began.

"Why would I text Brian if I forgot to text Heather?" Eric snapped.

"I don't know! Why would I text Heather?!"

"Because you're the mother-in-law."

Abby harrumphed and dug through her purse. "I'm calling Brian."

"And I'm calling Heather. Tell Brian to meet you at our apartment."

Abby did reach Brian. "Okay. I'll see you in about an hour and a half," he said.

Meanwhile Eric kept calling and texting Heather, but with no luck. "Why doesn't she answer?"

"Should I tell Brian to come to the airport?"

"But he won't have a car seat," Eric retorted. "Otherwise we could just get an Uber or Lyft. Maybe she's in the shower or something." He kept calling, but still Heather didn't pick up.

"Any friends with car seats?" Abby queried.

"No."

"Forget the car seat?"

Eric shot Abby an irritated look. "No!"

"Well, I'm going to give Brian a heads up that we may not be there when he gets to your house." Abby called Brian, but unsurprisingly he didn't pick up because he was driving. She just left a message and then watched Eric try to get a hold of Heather again. "I think there's smoke coming out of your phone."

"Ha, ha."

Abby's phone rang. "It's Brian," she announced as she took the call.

"It's rush hour and traffic's awful!" Brian fairly yelled. "Couldn't you have picked a better time to arrive?"

"Yeah, sure," Abby said coolly. "Like last week."

"Well, who knows when I'll get to the apartment."

"That isn't a problem. We still don't know where Heather is."

"Do you want me to go all the way to the airport?"

"No," Abby replied, looking over at Eric. "You don't have a car seat." Eric gave an approving nod. "Just be prepared that we may not be there when you arrive."

"That's because you'll die of old age before I get there," Brian grumbled. "If I don't have a stroke first."

"Calm down. You're not in a hurry. I'll keep you—"

"Eric!" Both Abby and Eric spun around to see who it was.

"Heather!" Eric ran towards her with Jillian.

"She's here!" Abby told Brian. "We'll see you in the city." She hung up and watched as Heather met her daughter for the first time.

Heather took Jillian into her arms and smothered her with kisses. "Look at her!" she said excitedly. "She's so beautiful!" Tears came down her cheeks as Eric put his arm around his wife. Abby wiped some tears away as well. Not just for the sight of Heather meeting her baby, but also for relief at finally getting home.

"I'll go get the car," Heather said hurriedly.

"Oh, let's walk," Abby replied. "Let's keep the family together."

"Okay," Heather laughed. "Although it would have been easier with a stroller."

"Well, that's in Poland," Eric sighed, shifting Jillian in his arms. "Our suitcases are in Ukraine and I can't remember where the car seat is. You did bring a car seat, didn't you?"

"Yes. You told me to, remember? Here, let me take Jillian."

Heather proudly carried her baby through the terminal and out into the parking garage. "Ooh, she's a big girl," Heather said, hitching Jillian up in the garage elevator. Soon Jillian was secure in her new car seat with Abby beside her as Heather guided the car round and round to the garage exit.

When they arrived at Eric and Heather's, Brian was outside waiting. They all hustled inside and Abby FaceTimed Paige so she could see her new niece. "Do you want to stay for lunch?" Heather asked Brian and Abby. "I think I can scrounge up something here."

"No thanks, dear. I just want to get home and sleep. And you and Eric need time alone with your daughter."

"I need time with a shower first!" Eric chuckled. "And then some sleep."

"I guess it's just me and Jillian, then," Heather grinned. "And I'm not complaining. At least today I'm not." She reached out to Abby. "Thank you for being such a wonderful grandmother and mother-in-law."

"You're welcome, dear," Abby replied, hugging her. "We'll talk about babysitting once I've rested a while."

"You're a glutton for punishment," Eric said.

"Jillian needs to keep up with her reggae," Abby winked.

Heather looked over at Eric with raised brows. "Mom's idea of suitable entertainment," Eric explained. Heather chuckled. They hugged and Abby and Brian left.

Heather never put Jillian down for the rest of the day. Holding her was the only way to make it real that her baby was here, safe and sound. At times she became very emotional, recalling the first weeks of Chloe's life, but mostly her tears were of joy that Eric and Jillian had made it home, safe and sound. True to his word, Eric stayed in bed most of the day, in turns napping and just laying there, blissful that his wife and daughter were bonding.

Jillian adapted quickly and easily into a routine, something this poor baby had not had since the first few days of her life. Eric went back to working some days at the office, but Heather decided to keep her maternity leave going for a few extra weeks. She hadn't lined up childcare yet and she was reluctant to leave her baby with anyone else, although they certainly needed money. Eric had made some calculations and the trip had cost about fifty percent more than they had budgeted. But he too was reluctant to leave Jillian with anyone else.

That night Abby slept better than she had in many years. She wasn't sure if it was because she was finally home safe and sound, or that she was just so exhausted. When she awoke late the next morning, she stretched out in bed and then felt a pang of loneliness, not having Jillian nearby. The bond between them felt different than the bond she had felt with Chloe because of the ordeal they went through. She sighed and shook it off. It would be different now, but not less. Abby got out of bed and wandered into the kitchen, finding that Brian had set out a lovely spread of lox and bagels. "Yum," she said to herself.

"Ready for your Earl Grey?"

Abby spun around, finding Brian looking far more groomed than he usually did that time of day. "Oh yes," she said, giving him a little kiss. "Can you imagine that I didn't even have one cup of tea this whole time because I couldn't figure out which milk was nonfat?"

"Yes, I can," Brian laughed.

Abby shrugged. "It wasn't as bad as it was giving up coffee in the 1980's."

"Did you start writing your book about your experiences?".

"A little," she smiled. "But it's not like I had much time to do that."

"Well, now you do."

Abby spent the next few days resting and meeting friends at her favorite café. The more she told the story, the closer she got to writing it all down. Finally, after a week or so of catching up with people, she decided to bring her computer to the café and see if she would get inspired to write. It didn't take long for her to get in a zone where she could block out the conversations around her. The words came easily and her fingers moved quickly, typing her story, or to be exact, Jillian's story. "This is easier than I thought it would be," she said to Brian when she got home.

"Good for you! Come see what I did today." Brian led Abby to a spare bedroom that had become an art studio for him. There on an easel was a large portrait of newborn Jillian.

"Wow! It's beautiful! Such an amazing likeness!"

"Pretty good for working from a cell phone picture," Brian agreed. "I jazzed up the composition a bit with color and texture." Abby starting humming "One Love" and Brian chuckled. "Yeah, something like that."

Abby continued humming as she snapped a picture of the portrait and sent it to Eric, Heather and Paige. "Now I just need to write a song about it and between us we will have covered a trifecta of the arts!"

Meanwhile in San Francisco, Heather dressed Jillian up in a sunny yellow pinafore with a matching bonnet tied under her chin. "You must be off to somewhere special," Eric said as his wife and daughter entered the kitchen.

"I think it's time Jillian met Chloe . . . and Jed, of course."

Eric nodded. "Do you want me to come with you?"

"If you want, but I'm okay to go alone." She smiled. "After all, Jed will be there too."

Eric thought for a minute. "I do have an appointment this morning, but I could cancel it."

Heather shrugged. "It's up to you."

Eric couldn't figure out whether Heather wanted him to go or not. It had always been so hard for her to go to the columbarium and see Chloe, but he also thought that maybe having Jillian would change that. And maybe it would be good for her to do this alone. "Well, I really shouldn't cancel the appointment. It could be a big commission."

"I'll be fine," Heather said, trying to sound assertive, but actually sounding hesitant.

When Heather arrived at the columbarium she noticed the parking lot was nearly full. That meant a service was going on. When she went inside she bumped into Jed at the door. He took her hand and smiled, studying her. She smiled back reassuringly and then started walking towards the stairs. Off to one side was a large photo of a boy about eight years old, and she almost stumbled, struck with the irony that today there would be a service for a child. She paused and held Jillian close, listening to an older woman give a eulogy.

"Sean was a teacher's delight, full of curiosity and spunk. Sometimes, maybe his spunk got a little out of hand." The crowd of people laughed. "He had a hard time reining in his eagerness and enthusiasm, but he was a good student." Her voice started to crack. "A friend to all and always helpful to those students who didn't grasp concepts as quickly as he did." She paused to gather herself together. "He was a special boy who will be greatly missed by all of us at school."

Heather choked back her own tears and continued to mount the stairs. She had envisioned the "meeting" between Jillian and Chloe to be difficult for her, but not this difficult. She hadn't expected such a visceral reminder of her own grief when she walked through the door. She touched the glass pane on Chloe's niche or "apartment" as she opened her mouth, but no words came out. She felt a hand on her shoulder and turned around to see Jed standing there. "Let me see this beautiful baby," he said.

Heather looked up at him, her eyes bright with tears. "I thought I could do this . . ."

"Would you like me to do the honors of introducing the two sisters?" he said.

Heather nodded and handed Jillian to him. She had kept Jed updated while Eric had been away, so he knew the whole story. "I guess I picked the wrong morning to come," she said tipping her head to the voices coming from the service downstairs.

"Oh, no," Jed replied. "You came at the perfect time—the perfect time to heal." Jed held Jillian up to the door and said, "This is your sister Chloe. Like me, you'll never meet her in person, but you'll love her just the same."

Heather muffled a sob. "Thank you, Jed."

He started to sing "Let it Go" to Chloe and Heather managed to join in. When he finished he looked at Jillian, who stared at him wide eyed. "Someday you'll be joining us in song, too."

"I can't imagine what she'll insist on singing," Heather smiled as she wiped her cheek. "There will be something new that we'll have to learn."

Jed started in on "The Garden Song," but his voice trailed off about a third of the way through. "I think we need a new song," he murmured.

"Yes, I think you're right," Heather replied, studying Jillian who was studying Jed. "The garden has bloomed."

Jed looked over at Heather and flashed a smile. "What a wonderful sight . . .what a wonderful . . ." He then took a deep breath. "I see trees of green . . . red roses too . . ."

"I see them bloom," Heather wavered "for me and for you . . ."

www.ingramcontent.com/pod-product-compliance
Lightning Source LLC
Chambersburg PA
CBHW021230190726
48289CB00005B/1250